MOMENT OF IMPACT

Moment of Impact

A Lucas Caine Thriller

CALEB WYGAL

Grand Strand Publishing

ALSO BY CALEB WYGAL

Mytle Beach Mystery Novels
The Brass Key (Short Story Prequel)
Death on the Boardwalk
Death Washes Ashore
Death on the Golden Mile
Death on the Causeway
Death at Tidal Creek

Lucas Caine Novels
Moment of Impact
A Murder in Concord
Blackbeard's Lost Treasure
The Search for the Fountain of Youth

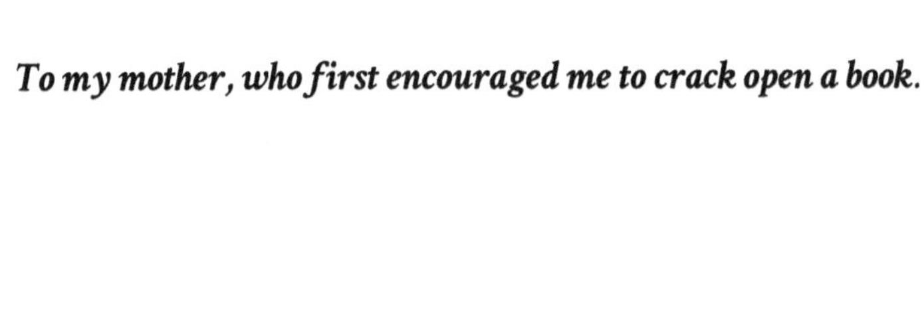

To my mother, who first encouraged me to crack open a book.

PROLOGUE

Major things that happen in a person's life are rare things. You can go along smooth sailing for years, and then BAM! Something major happens you are unprepared for. Or, sometimes, you can see where something is lurking just beyond the horizon. It is like a storm cloud approaching.

You can see it coming, but you cannot just tell it to go away. You still must prepare yourself for what is coming.

Believe me. I know how something unexpected can change a person's life. I also know how a foreseeable event can change a person's life as well. How we handle these changes can shape your life for the present and for the future.

Normally, we have no power over these life-changing events. You have to learn to live or cope with these life-altering events. The fact is that we do not have a choice in what happens.

We must deal with the events that face us whether we like it or not, or suffer the consequences...

PART ONE

CHAPTER ONE

The weather was perfect. The sun was high in the azure sky, covered by the occasional passing cloud. Passing clouds brought a slow, pleasant breeze with them. The temperature was warm, but not so warm that you had to find some shade to hide in.

I looked to my left and saw a vacant, sandy white beach stretching for miles. I could also look down to my right and see the same scene repeat itself. Behind us, there were no high-rise resorts or hotels. Just a line of lush, thick trees.

We had total privacy.

We sat in two comfortable beach chairs that sat beside each other. Behind us lay a blanket with remnants of a picnic lunch. The chairs were close enough to the water where the tide lapped against our feet, ending their long journey that started far out into the ocean.

I could not have asked to have a better companion to be sitting alongside me. Elizabeth looked stunning in her two-piece black swimsuit with a flowery blue sarong flowing over a pair of well-tanned legs. She had her blonde hair tied back with a few loose strands of hair fluttering back and forth across her face.

The banter between us easy, with varied topics moving from school to our past to our future to things as mundane as a debate on what type of ice cream that we liked best. Laughter abounded.

I don't think I have ever been as happy in my entire life. Her smile put me in heaven.

Then, in the silkiest voice that she had, she said, "Lucas, wake up, time for school."

What?

"Lucas, wake up!" I heard through the obscurity. This time, the voice was not very silky or smooth.

In an instant, I was plunged back into the real world. I rolled over, away from the voice of my mom, and shut my eyes together tighter, hoping that I could stay on that beach. Then, she ripped the sheet away, revealing me in nothing but a pair of boxers. How embarrassing.

"I said, get up! I've been yelling at you to wake up for fifteen minutes." With that, she stormed out of the room, slamming the door behind her.

"But I was having such a nice dream," I said to the closed door.

CHAPTER TWO

Jake Schofield lay on his bed, looking up at the darkened ceiling above his head. He looked over at the luminescent dial on his alarm clock sitting on his nightstand. 4:33 a.m. Jake had now been staring at the same darkened ceiling for about six and a half hours. When that alarm goes off at 7:00 a.m., he would begin his new life.

Jake's parents had bought the spot of land that his new house sits on a mere two months ago. At that time, this 'spot of land' was the only vacant lot left on the main road in the little community of Mt. Lookout. His parents were in a hurry to move. They wanted a new house in a hurry, but they did not want to settle for any cheap housing like a trailer or doublewide.

"Those are for people with less money than us," his dad, Carl, had told him when they were on the modular home lot. "No, son, we can buy one of these normal-looking homes that the salesman says can be built from start to finish in about a month and a half. That way, if we have to move again, it won't be at a great loss."

Jake looked at the one- and two-story model homes around him and did not think that what his dad had just told him would be possible.

Jake turned into a believer over the next several weeks.

A little less than two months after Jake and his family stood on that model home site, his father received the keys to their complete home. Even though it had taken just a short time to build it, his parents thought the house looked incredible. Jake did not have an opinion of his new home.

Jake looked at his alarm clock for what must have been the hundredth time this night. The glowing red letters displayed 4:47.

Jake was restless on this night because when that alarm clock went off, he would get ready for his first day of school at his new high school. For many reasons, he was very nervous. His unease didn't stem from the typical worries of a normal teenager starting at a new school in the middle of a year. His thoughts weren't on whether he could make friends or find his way around school.

Other reasons brought him to Mt. Lookout, WV.

He hoped no one would find out why he was here.

Jake and his parents, Cherie and Carl, went to the local high school in nearby Summersville a week earlier to enroll Jake. They met the Principal, Mrs. Penninger, and the football coach, Coach Dunlap, on that day.

The school was in a long, one-story brown brick building just off the main highway. To Jake's parents, it seemed like a nice little school. The schools Jake attended in the past were much larger than Nicholas County High School. Jake knew he would have to adjust to a smaller school.

Coach Dunlap seemed excited about Jake joining the school. At his previous school, Jake started at defensive back, and he could join the football team. The Grizzles, as the school referred to themselves, struggled with a new quarterback under center. Jake could help right away.

The school was small and had a modest budget to go with it. Coach Dunlap wore several hats. Among them, he was the head football coach, Vice-Principal, and he taught a history class during the mornings. He was a very busy man. His manic personality reflected on that.

Mrs. Penninger, on the other hand, was not as excited to have Jake attending her school. She came from the old style of teaching and disciplining. If she had her way, she would require all students to wear drab, depressing uniforms, and would allow teachers discipline their students with the sharp rap of a yardstick. She was also concerned about what brought the Schofield family to Nicholas County, but she couldn't keep Jake from attending her school.

He looked over at the clock one last time and rubbed his eyes. 5:01 a.m. He supposed he would try to close his eyes for a while. With any luck, he could get an hour of sleep before the dreaded alarm went off.

Then he would begin a new chapter in his life. Hopefully, for the better.

CHAPTER THREE

By the time I finished my morning routine—brush teeth, shower, and quick shave—we were running behind. The night of dream-filled sleep left me groggy. I don't have vivid dreams very often, but when I do, it seems like I take a little longer to get going the next morning. Maybe, sometimes, I wish I could have stayed in whatever movie reel my mind played the night before.

I have a few traveling companions that I chauffeur to and from school every day. My younger brother Blake is a grade below me in school. There are the brothers. My neighbors, Brian and Allen, get a free ride every day. They always fight and snap at each other. The last passenger was Stone. He lives a little way up the street. The five of us have been close friends for as long as I can remember.

When I reached my car, Brian and Allen were already getting into it.

Well, they were not getting into the car, but into it with each other. It was more Brian picking on Allen than anything else was.

"Stop it, Brian!" Allen yelled while Brian was sitting on Allen's back and had one of Allen's arms wrapped around behind his back in a very uncomfortable-looking position. "Get off!"

Brian laughed like a hyena. It was easy to see that he was enjoying his morning.

They have been our neighbors since I was about one-year-old. We've known them for as long as I can remember. They live in a double-wide a scant fifty yards from our front door. We hang out a lot and play many sports together. They fight like Hatfield's and McCoy's. They may not show it, but they do have a strong bond. They would do just about anything for each other.

Allen is sort of a runt. He is barely over five feet tall and still has a lot of baby fat on him. He has short light blond hair and a red blotchy birthmark above his left ear. His brother, Brian, is almost a polar opposite. He is roughly six feet tall, dark hair, glasses, and muscular.

"All right pud. I'll get off ya."

Brian removed himself from Allen, but not before twisting his arm a little more. Brian was a senior at our school while Allen and I were sophomores. I found it interesting how they still fought like a couple of elementary school kids.

"Hey guys," Brian said to us, "I see you overslept again."

My hair was still drying from where I took my shower, and as it dries, it rather has that effect that you get when you stick your finger in a light socket, it stands straight up. I think that it has to do with the late summer early fall humidity.

"Yeah, shut up. How are you guy's doin'?" I asked, while opening the driver's side door.

"We're okay." Brian answered, opening his door after I had all the doors unlocked.

"My arm is hurtin'," Allen replied, emitting another laugh from Brian.

I shook my head at the two brothers. "C'mon, we need to hurry. Everyone in."

Brian rode shotgun. Blake and Allen piled into the backseat. I pulled out of the driveway taking care to check and see if there were any cars coming down the hill behind our massive weeping willow tree, which hangs out over the road.

I live in a split-level home on a little one-lane road called Mt. Lookout Rd. near Summersville. We have a swimming pool that has a tarp over it. Unfortunately, that season is over. There is a basketball hoop in our gravel driveway between a well-landscaped lawn that my parents have spent years cultivating.

I earned my driver's license the day that I turned sixteen. After that, my parents bought me a little red Chevy to drive to and from school. It's not the nicest car by any stretch of the imagination, but most of the kids in my school still must ride the bus, or, like my passengers, hitch a ride with someone with an automobile.

We drove a short distance up the road, where I pulled into Stone's driveway. I honked the horn, and Stone came through the door and out to my car. He pushed Blake into the middle between him and Allen and closed the door.

"Morning ladies," Stone said, piling into the backseat.

Stone is the type of person other people gravitated towards. He is one of the most popular people in school, even though he is an underclassman. Everyone defers to him in any situation, whether it is picking teams during gym class, class projects, or whatever. Everyone waits to see what he is going to do, then the other people will most times follow suit. I am not that way with him, and that is why I think he likes me so much. I will not suck up to him like some of our other classmates.

Stone is, and this hurts to say, what we typically refer to as a "ladies' man". He has all the physical features that make a person popular with the ladies. He is a little above average height, has blue eyes, and muscular build, one of the most athletic guys in school, and has a glowing personality. He seems to have it all put together.

Sometimes I wish I had it as easy as Stone with girls.

Stone and I started talking about the football game that we played last Friday while I drove. We played against the powerhouse Woodrow Wilson in Beckley. To keep a long story short, they crushed us. We had to play at their place in Beckley, a large town about thirty miles to the south of Summersville. Since our team is young, and their team went to the state finals last year, it was not a pretty game. I did not play well, throwing three interceptions.

I'm still a little sore from the beating I took.

It was a difficult, but not unexpected, loss. I spent the weekend wallowing in my own misery. Was I too hard on myself? Probably. The loss motivated me to improve. I intended to speak with my coaches about what I could have done better last week and have a strong practice after class this afternoon.

When we got a little way up the road, we came upon a home that had been under construction, but now looked finished. A construction company began clearing off the plot of land on which this new home sat several months ago. For a while, nothing seemed to happen. The lot lay bare and ugly. Then one day, a crew poured the foundation, followed by a shipment of construction materials a few days later. After that, the home went up quickly and looked completed sometime last week.

It is a nice two-story Cape Cod with white siding and dark blue shutters to accent the white covered porch running the length of the front of the house. It sits up on a hill, so it gives the effect to passers-bye of being a bigger house than what it is. The yard around the house still looks like a construction zone. The ground does not have any grass yet, and there are still remnants of discarded scraps of wood and siding all over the dirt yard.

As we passed the house, I noticed for the first time a couple of cars in the driveway. I saw a kid that looked to be about our age getting into the passenger side of the minivan. He had on a long black overcoat concealing a pair of black pants.

"Do you all know anything about this family that just moved in?" I asked the group. A new family moving into our small community was an enormous source of gossip for a few weeks for most people.

"No," was the response that I received from everyone. That was weird. More often than not, somebody knew something. Nobody spoke much the rest of the way to school. Everybody in the car seemed to be lost in the post-weekend melancholy that afflicts most kids as the free time was over and it was back to school for another week.

We pulled out of Mt. Lookout Rd. onto the busy highway of U.S. Route 19. While not an interstate, Route 19 is one of the main highways linking northern to southern West Virginia.

The interstates that go through our state travel through the capital city of Charleston.

Charleston was not exactly in the center of the state, so those that traveled interstate heading north or going south, had to go well out of their way to do that if they are heading to Pittsburgh from Florida. Route 19 conveniently connected two interstates together, cutting several hours from any trip.

In the mid-1990's, the state provided funds to expand Route 19 to four lanes. Once completed, travelers flowed through Summersville. While on the well-traveled road, it was common to see license plates from as far north as Ontario, Canada, and as far south as Florida. Most of the time, you see these license plates as they sped past you in the left lane.

Because of the increased traffic through the corridor, Summersville has gone through an economic boon. The addition of several casual and fast-food restaurants and hotels brought hundreds of jobs to the town. The increased taxes allowed local government to upgrade facilities and enhance programs.

There are no other major towns within thirty miles on either side of Summersville. Really, it was well positioned as an attractive rest area and the many dining places invite travelers to stop and throw some money into Summersville's growing economy. That is a benefit to living in a 'fast food nation.' People hurry so much that they do not allow time to stop and enjoy a nice sit-down dinner when they travel. Therefore, when people drove through an isolated area such as Summersville and saw a convenient way to get a quick bite to eat, they would stop.

This proved beneficial for the police department as well. While speed traps are supposed to be illegal, the Summersville

Police Department has a scheme that seems, well, shady. The speed limit along most of Route 19 is sixty-five miles per hour. When you enter the town limits of Summersville, the speed limit plummets to fifty.

Peaks and valleys characterize the stretch of Route 19 that cuts through Summersville. The road will go up one large hill, fall down the backside of that hill, and then up again repeating the process another several times as the road meanders through the town. This leads to many blind spots for unaware travelers.

Many of the people traveling through Summersville for the first time barely take notice of the lower speed limit. So, when they crest a hill going sixty-five to seventy miles per hour, the cops lie in wait with their speed guns trained on the top of the hill and get them every time. One kid in my class is the son of the sheriff, and he says that the money brought in from all of those speeding tickets is more than Summersville brings in from all the other types of tourism that the Summersville area offers. That includes Summersville Lake.

I make sure that I obey the speed limit as I pass through town. I haven't been pulled over since I've had my license, but I know some friends who have. I don't want to join them in that club.

On the main stretch of 19 that goes through Summersville, neon lights are everywhere. It is an ugly part of town, but if you get off Route 19 to Broad Street, you will enter an established downtown with a large, elegant, stone courthouse, many old, red-bricked buildings, and a little park. Most people never see this peaceful, quaint part of Summersville. If they did, I am sure that more people would stop and stay in our town instead of just passing through it.

CHAPTER FOUR

I go to an average sized school for our state. A gymnasium climbs above the roof of the rest of the one-storied school. The acronym for Nicholas County High School, NCHS, dominates the side of the gymnasium facing the main road. There is a baseball field behind the school and a practice football field beside it. The actual football stadium is about a mile back down Route 19 at Veterans Memorial Park.

This morning, we are a little late getting to school. This was normal.

We pulled into the student parking lot and got out of our car and heard what we hoped was the warning bell for the kids to get to their homerooms. The bell for the actual start of class comes five minutes after the warning bell.

When we approached the entrance of the school, I saw the kid getting out of the minivan from the new home in Mt. Lookout. Up close, he looked to be a few inches shorter than me, with blond hair slicked back. He went in the doors ahead of us and went directly to the principal's office on the right.

As we entered the school, we went into the cafeteria, or as the faculty of the school referred to it, the Commons Area. The principal's office sat to our immediate right. Just past the office door, there was a double door. This led to one of two main hall-ways filled with classrooms. There is another door about fifty feet down the wall on that same side. It leads to the other hall-way filled with classrooms. To the left of the Commons Area, on the wall where the front entrance is, is a hallway that leads to the auditorium and the band room. In the back-left corner of the Commons Area is a short hallway leading to the gym and the faculty parking lot. The Commons Area is the hub of the school.

Blake and Brian went to different doors than the rest of us. Stone, Allen, and I all have the same homeroom. We entered the entrance beside the principal's office and went to Mrs. Gibson's room halfway down the hall. We did not have time to go to our lockers before the second bell rang, which told all students that they had better be in a classroom somewhere.

Mrs. Gibson usually came in just as the morning bell rang. This morning was no different.

"Good morning, class," she said, hustling into the room. "Everybody get to your seats."

Those who weren't already seated, me included, rushed to their seats. I took my assigned seat behind Stone and in front of Allen, near the window.

I am lucky enough to have the same homeroom as Elizabeth, the girl from my dream this morning. The bad part is that he sits on the far side of the classroom. This makes conversation with her difficult. I have another good friend, Ashley, who sits behind her.

The classroom has the usual big chalkboard covering the entire front wall. There were a few supply cabinets in each of the back corners of the room. Right now, since it was autumn, the room had a Thanksgiving theme to it. There were cardboard cutouts of turkeys, cornucopias, and scarecrows scattered on the walls throughout the room.

Mrs. Gibson is one of the geography teachers for our grade. She has turkeys and pilgrims mixed in with maps of the United States and of the world.

She took roll call. Everyone was present. She tells the students they can work on their homework or study for a test if they have any that might come later in the day. I didn't have anything to do but sit quietly in my chair and try to recall the dream that I was having this morning.

A knock came at the door. Mrs. Gibson stood up from her desk and went over to check on the visitor. Whoever was at the door whispered a few words to Mrs. Gibson. She then stood aside and let the new kid that we saw this morning enter the room. A small murmur of anticipation went through the classroom.

"Class, I'd like to introduce to you our new student, Jake, ah, Schofield." She paused for a moment to let him wave at everyone. "Jake comes to us from Charlotte, NC." There was one open seat left in the classroom, and it was in front of Elizabeth, near the door.

Mrs. Gibson turned to Jake. "As your homeroom teacher, I will assign you your locker. Nobody in the office assigned you a locker, did they?"

He shook his head.

She scanned the room. It looked like she was going to delegate one of us to show him to a locker and maybe give him a tour of the school. Going on this idea, I tried to sink down in my seat, which is difficult, because all the desks in the school were undersized for me.

I'm not much of a ninja, and her eyes locked on mine.

"Lucas. Do you think you could show Jake here where his locker is? I'll give him a combination to one in a minute and then show him around the school?"

No, I immediately thought, but responded, "Okay."

I got up out of my chair and went up to the front of the room, while Mrs. Gibson assigned Jake a locker number.

"Let's go," I said, leading the new guy out of the classroom.

"Remember, Lucas, you've got less than twenty minutes before the bell rings. So don't dawdle in the gym for too long," Mrs. Gibson said as we headed out the door.

She knows the way I think.

CHAPTER FIVE

"Your name is Jake, huh?" I asked. He nodded. "I'm Lucas. Nice to meet you."

I extended my hand to him, which he gripped with the strength of a dead fish. He was a few inches shorter than I was, which would put him at about average height. He has blond hair and green eyes sitting underneath a pair of well-trimmed eyebrows. This struck me as odd. I do not think that I have ever seen a guy with trimmed eyebrows. Maybe it was from growing up in a small town. It must be a city thing. Or maybe I just don't spend much time checking out other guy's eyebrows.

"Nice to meet you too," he said without emotion as he released my hand, and we started the short walk down the hall to where our assigned lockers were. He didn't seem thrilled to be here. I wondered if he was missing his old school right about now.

"What locker number did Mrs. Gibson give you?" I asked him as we arrived at the bank of lockers assigned to our homeroom.

He looked down at the little post-it note that Mrs. Gibson had given him, "Number 315."

I frowned. "That's the one right next to mine. Damn."

He looked at me. "Why? What's the matter with that?"

"Oh, it's got nothing to do with you," I responded. "It's just that at the beginning of the year, when Mrs. Gibson assigned lockers, I was the last one in line. When she reached the bottom of her locker list, she had a couple left she did not assign. I looked at her the paper with the locker combinations on it and memorized the combination to your locker. You know, for extra storage."

He gave me a sideways look. "Extra storage?"

"Yeah, a guy can't have too much space, you know."

"What am I supposed to do now?"

"It's not you that has to do anything. It's me. I guess that I'll have to figure out a place to put all my junk that's in that locker. It's your locker now," I said, spinning the combination to his locker.

"Oh. Thanks, I think. Look, I'm not going to have much to put in there for a few days, so you don't have to clear everything out right now."

"Thanks for the offer," I told him, pulling some of my things out of his new locker, "but I'll be alright. I guess I can put stuff in my locker in the gym."

Another sideways look. "You have *three* lockers?" he asked with a little sarcasm mixed into his voice. This is the first time that I had noticed any hint of emotion from the guy.

"*Had* three lockers," I explained, as if to a little child. "A guy has to have his space."

I showed him how to work the combination on his locker and then started transferring some items in his new locker over to mine.

"Are you ready?" I asked as I picked up the few other books I set aside.

"I should be. I didn't have too much to put in there, anyway."

"Oh, you will. I'm going to show you the gym first. That way, I can take these books down there. Let's head back out to the Commons Area." I explained to him the general layout of the school as we walked down the hall. He asked me where I was from.

"I'm from around here. I've lived in the Summersville area my entire life. I don't live too far from where you just built your new house in Mt. Lookout," I said as we walked down the empty hallway.

"How do you know where I live?"

"I saw you getting into your van this morning."

"Oh, okay," he said, going quiet again before changing the subject. "This town seems kind of quiet. In the places I've lived, it's unusual not to hear a siren every five minutes. I've usually lived in big cities where there's always something happening. They always filled the local news with murders, apartment fires, and robberies."

It sounded as though he was trying to impress this small-town guy of all the big places that he has lived before. I didn't care where he came from.

"Yeah, around here, when you hear a siren, it's gossip for about a week."

"Wow."

"This room coming up is Mrs. Dooley's room. She's the world history teacher for the freshmen. My little brother is in there somewhere, Blake. He's a little pain in the butt. Do you have any brothers or sisters?"

"No," he responded, "I'm an only child."

"That'd be nice," I said. "That kid can be such a pain sometimes."

"I wish I had a brother," Jake said.

"You can have mine if you want."

He laughed for the first time. "No, I don't think so, not if he's as much of a pain as you claim he is. My dad works for the government, and we have to move around all the time. It's hard for me to keep friends that way. At least if I had a brother, I would always have someone to talk to."

We got to the end of the hallway and made our way right into the Commons Area. I said, "You've already been in there at the principal's office. We're going to cut across the Commons Area here to get to the gym hallway." He nodded. "Over to the left there, you have one set of bathrooms across from the auditorium. There are also some vending machines over there."

We cut across the empty cafeteria to the little hallway that led to the gymnasium. The sounds of pots and pans clattered in the kitchen. The smell of bread being prepared for lunch wafted through the open space. We went into the gym where the two gym teachers were setting up ping-pong tables.

One of the gym teachers, Coach Nixon, called over to me. "You're a little early, Lucas. Go back to class."

"I'm not early, coach. I'm just showing this new guy, Jake, around," I said, gesturing to my partner.

"Hey, Jake," Nixon said to him. "Are you going to be at practice today?"

"Of course," I said.

"I wasn't talking to you, boy. I was talking to Jake."

I raised my eyebrows and looked over at Jake, who was nodding his head.

"Good. Good," he said to Jake's silent affirmative. He switched his stern gaze to me. "I don't know if Jake told you, but he started at free safety at his school in North Carolina. I believe they were the number one ranked school in the nation. Right Jake?" He nodded. Nixon continued, "He's going to step in right away to take over the position from Brandon."

Brandon is the rather untalented and undersized starting free-safety on our team.

"Watch your passes in practice and make sure he doesn't show you up and pick one off."

It was Jake's turn to look at me in surprise. "I didn't know you played quarterback."

I lucked my way into being the starting quarterback on our high school football team. I am not the best. I'm learning. I can manage a game fairly well and let the playmakers on the team go to work. I simply try not to embarrass myself. I got the quarterback job because the senior who was supposed to be quarterback blew out his knee and can't play this year. I was the backup, now I am the starter.

"I didn't know you played safety," I said.

"Touché."

"Lucas is our starter. And he's a pretty decent quarterback at that. He could be better if studied up on game film instead of studying up on biology every night. Don't tell Coach Wheeler

I said that either," he said, pointing a finger at me, but with a smile on his face.

Coach Wheeler is my biology teacher and the assistant coach on the team. Jake looked at me with a new level of respect etched on his face. Leave it to Coach Nixon to puff me up in front of other members of the team. That way, when I lose the game because of an interception that I threw or a fumble that I coughed up, the ridicule is even worse.

"I've gotta take some stuff and put it into my locker back here, then finish showing him around," I said to Coach Nixon, trying to get out of the conversation.

"Okay. Jake, Lucas, I'll see you boys back here in a few minutes," he said to me as we walked through a door leading to the locker rooms.

"I'm the teacher's aide during the next period," I explained. "It's pretty cool. I get to play all the basketball that I want, and I don't have to do any of the warm-up exercises."

"Yeah, an hour and a half gym class sounds pretty cool to me. I've got gym for first period too." He changed the subject again. "What's the deal with this 'block' scheduling you all have at this school?"

4x4 block scheduling is a simple concept. During a day, you have four hour and half-long classes, with a forty-five-minute lunch in the middle of the day. You take these four classes for one semester, and then you take four different classes the next semester. The idea behind this is you have more time for the teachers to instruct the kids in one sitting. This way, students don't have to worry about keeping track of seven different subjects all the time, therefore, less homework. In addition, students learn eight different subjects in a year, instead of seven. I like it. However, parents grumbled that their kids were coming home with *more* homework now.

I went back to the gym locker room and put the books into the smaller locker that I have there. I had to shove aside my football equipment to get everything to fit. I looked at my watch and told Jake that we had to hurry. The homeroom period was almost up. I gave him a hurried tour of the rest of the school now that my personal agenda was finished and showed him where his other three classes were outside of the gym.

We made back to Mrs. Gibson's room almost at the end of the homeroom period.

"Thanks for showing me around," Jake said.

"You're welcome," I replied. "You need anything. Let me know."

"I'm sure there will be something I'll need. I'll let you know." The bell sounded. We looked at each other. "Ready to head back to the gym?"

"Always. It's a nice group of kids you'll be with. Cute girls too."

He smiled. "Well, that's something to look forward to."

CHAPTER SIX

When it comes to the lunch period, I dislike eating what the school prepares. When lunch hour comes, I don't have to wait in line to get my food. I just brown bag it every day. Because I do not have to stand in line to get lunch, I am usually one of the first guys to arrive at the table where I normally sit.

Jake had brought his lunch as well, and I offered him a seat at my table, where he sat across from me.

All the other friends in my group of friends ate the school's lunch. I could not stand the stuff. I am a very picky eater. I do not like to eat chicken, salads, and other 'weird' stuff. At this point in my life, all I basically eat is peanut butter and jelly sandwiches, snack cakes, cookies, pizza, and mac n' cheese. I eat no vegetables and very little meat. My parents tell people that is why I got so much taller than all the other kids, because what I primarily ate was Mac n' Cheese. They also say that my diet is why I am so skinny; I don't eat a lot of protein, which would stick to my ribs.

Coach Nixon says that if I were to eat a healthier diet and bulk up, that by the end of my senior year, I might have some colleges' approach me about being their quarterback. Blah, blah, blah. I have no dreams about playing quarterback after high school. My true love in sports is in basketball. If I play college ball in any sport, the only one that I would like to do is basketball.

"So, how do you like it so far?" I asked Jake between bites of my sandwich.

"Not bad," he said. He nodded his head as he unwrapped his sandwich. "You all seem all right, so let me ask you, is there anyone I should beware of or stay away from?"

I raised my eyebrows. That's an odd question.

"You should probably avoid half of the girls in the school," I said, looking around the cafeteria. "They'll tell on you over the smallest things, and if you do something to one of them, they'll all know it in about ten seconds. Gossip is big in this school amongst the girls. They think that every guy in this school should worship the ground that they walk on. I don't understand girls, or even pretend to understand them."

"Got a girlfriend?" he asked. I shook my head. It seemed Jake had already been on the lookout. "I've seen a few girls that stand out to me. How about that Elizabeth girl that I'm sitting in front of in homeroom? She's kind of hot. What do you think of her?"

I did not like the idea of this guy talking to Elizabeth. I have seen his schedule, so I know that they both have the same afternoon classes. So I lied a little, "Oh her, she's the worst of them all. I would avoid her at all costs. You both have the same classes in the afternoon."

"How do you know that?"

"Both of us have the same art class at the end of the day. I sit next to Elizabeth during that class, so I know she has the same algebra class that you do next period." I explain.

"Really? That's cool," he said. "She seems kind of nice to me."

"Oh no, she's the devil. Trust me."

"Okay. I'll take your word for it," he said, not sounding convinced.

By this time, my friends had received their lunch and started taking their seats. Stone and Allen sat on either side of me. Eric and William sat over next to Jake. I am related to these two guys. They all introduced themselves quickly before digging into their food.

"What junk are they serving you all today?" I asked to the newcomers.

"Pizza," William said. I have mentioned earlier that one thing that I will eat is pizza. However, this pizza was gross. They put ground up hamburger and put it *underneath* the cheese. That makes it very inedible to me. I like hamburgers too. I just do not like to mix my food up. I don't like for food on my dinner plates to touch each other.

"I don't know how you all can eat that stuff," I said, finishing my peanut butter and jelly sandwich.

"You're so weird sometimes," Allen said, stabbing at his pizza with a fork.

"You're one to talk booger eater."

Everyone but Jake laughed at this little inside joke.

When we were in Elementary School, Allen liked to pick and then eat his boogers. He stopped doing that a couple of years ago, though we have not forgotten. Everybody picks on Allen. Around here, if you do not have a sense of humor or cannot take a joke, you will not get along too well. Allen is one of those rare exceptions. He can make jokes, but he cannot take one. He gets flaming mad anytime that anyone says anything about him. My brother is the same way.

As lunch progressed, Jake seemed to get along pretty well. He would speak when spoken too and make brief comments here and there. He seemed to be a funny guy when he said something. He didn't not talk much, but I attributed that to this being his first day of school here and just feeling everybody out.

Jake finished his lunch at about the same time that I finished mine. "Do you want to go over to the gym?" I asked.

"What for?" he said, answering my question with a question. He turned around and looked in the general direction of the gym.

"During lunch, the teachers open the gym so kids who aren't eating lunch will have something to do. I usually go in there after I eat and shoot a few hoops. Play any basketball?" I asked.

He shrugged his shoulders and said, "I play a little."

When we reached the gym, there were about fifty kids running around on the different courts playing pickup games. The teachers had the two main baskets down, as well as two others on each side of the gym. The seniors were playing over at one end of the court. They do not let any underclassmen play with them. The juniors were playing on the other main goal at the other end of the gym, and the freshmen and sophomores have to play at the other four goals around the gym.

I saw Blake struggling to put up a shot against a boy twice his size over on one end of the court. I laughed. He is still too short to play basketball, in my opinion.

I walked over to the court where the juniors were playing as someone lost a ball out of bounds. I grabbed the ball and threw it to my friend Aaron on the court.

"Thanks man," he said. "Hey, we need one more. Want to play?"

"Sure," I responded. It's not every day an underclassman gets to play on one of the main courts during lunch. "Sorry," I muttered to Jake, then headed onto the court.

I had a few nice scoring plays, particularly against a guy who was a little bigger than myself. When the game was over, I walked over to where Jake was watching the game.

"That was a good-looking move that you put on that guy," he said. "Nice."

Coach Wheeler pulled lunch duty in the gym. He had been going around and collecting the basketballs from everyone, signifying that lunch has ended. He walked over to where Jake and I were standing near the exit and overheard what Jake said to me.

"Yeah, that was a nice move you put on Jason there, Lucas." He agreed with Jake. "If you keep improving, and don't get hurt during football season, we might let you try out for the Varsity team this year. Now go. Don't be late for class."

"Thanks coach!" I said to him with my biggest smile of the day. "I won't be late."

I turned to look for Jake. He was gone, and I guessed he had already gone to his first class of the afternoon. I rushed to my locker to get my books and then ran for Coach Wheeler's biology class.

I was only slightly late.

CHAPTER SEVEN

Biology class was a breeze. Coach Wheeler gave us a famous not-so-pop quiz. This meant that he warned us yesterday at the end of class that we might expect a quiz on that day's lesson. Translation: definite pop quiz tomorrow.

I'm like many of the so-called jocks. When I can, I try to take a class one of the football, basketball or baseball coaches conducts. I do it because I had already developed some sort of positive rapport with them before I ever stepped into one of their classrooms. Whereas, with any other non-coach type of teacher, most of the time, I likely hadn't met them beforehand. They didn't know me and sometimes that led to trouble.

It helped to get preferential treatment from the athletic coaches. It's not that I'm lazy or anything, I just liked to get a break occasionally.

After Biology class, I have my favorite class of any over the years: art class. I surprise people when I tell them that my favorite subject was art. Most would think I would say gym class or math, where I always scored near the top of the class.

No, I would tell them, art class was my preferred choice. I have been drawing pictures and cartoons ever since I was a very little kid. I found it to be one of the most fulfilling things I do. I always felt like I had accomplished something when I created a work of art.

Not that I just *draw* pictures. It is that I think I did it very well and I am proud of it. I have won every art contest I have entered since I was in Junior High. Last year, I won the biggest contest in the county and had my picture sent to hang in the state capital building. I am most proud in my life at this point of that achievement.

Mr. Eagle was my art teacher this year. He's a Grizzly Adams of a man. He's several inches taller than any student, including myself, and carries around an extra hundred pounds. He wore big, thick-framed glasses that we think he has had since the '60's. His most notable feature, though, was his very long and very red beard. Hence the nickname: Grizzly Adams.

Another thing that made this art class a little extra special is that Elizabeth Evans was in it. The class had several tables scattered around the room as opposed to desks. I sat across from Elizabeth at the same table. Sitting beside me was a guy named Arnie, and beside Elizabeth sat a girl named Mary Jane.

Sometimes having Elizabeth sitting across the table distracts me from my work. I will sit in my chair and stare at her while she her head was down working on the art project of the day. I sometimes forgot I even had an assignment.

I've known Elizabeth for as long as I can remember. We grew up down the street from each other. I go over to her house to do things with her older brother, Eric. I have been around her for a long time and have been infatuated or in love with her the entire time.

I must admit that I have never had a girlfriend. I always hoped Elizabeth would ask me to be her boyfriend. I don't have the courage to ask her myself.

I learned it doesn't work that way with her. Elizabeth was not shy when it came to the opposite sex. However, she was not used to making the first move. She's so pretty that guys come to her. If I expected her to make the first move towards any relationship between us, I could wait a long, long time.

Elizabeth was the most popular girl in our class. She has been ever since we graduated from elementary school to middle school and added hundreds of students to our class.

She had a way of keeping the spotlight on her without being a diva. She's down-to-earth and doesn't pretend to be better than everyone else where other girls with her qualities might. She joined the cheerleading squad as soon as she could and quickly worked her way up to head cheerleader after everyone saw her enthusiasm, athleticism, and leadership that she displayed during the first couple of weeks of tryouts.

Not content to be just a cheerleader, she is also the elected vice-president of our class. When she ran for the position, she did not even have to lobby for any votes. She won the election without having to lift a finger. She threw her name into the hat, put up a few flyers around the school, and won by a landslide. She really could have been president of the class had she wanted.

She has high cheekbones and dark blonde hair to go along with her slender, athletic build. Her family is proud of their Irish heritage, but she has the looks of a Greek Goddess. Her hairstyle has changed many times over the years. In one season, it could be very long, and then she would cut almost all of it off. Then she would wear it short and curly, or long and curly. Long and curly has been my favorite over the years. This is her current hairstyle. The only thing average about her was her height.

While this is the boilerplate description about any girl who is a main character in any story. I wouldn't describe her in this fashion if she wasn't like every dream girl that you read about in a book.

The only time that I ever strayed from having a crush on Elizabeth would be when I briefly had a little, tiny crush on her best friend Ashley. She's the girl that sits behind her in our homeroom. I considered her one of my closest friends as well. This was a couple of years ago. I thought maybe she liked me, so I developed a small interest in her. Nothing ever came of it, though.

Ashley was also in this class, but unfortunately, she was stuck sitting at a table on the other side of the room. This isn't the only class I have with Ashley, besides homeroom. She also has gym class the same period that I'm a teacher's aide, so I still get to talk to her a few times a day.

I have a few other good friends in this class, which makes it easy to come here and enjoy it. Jake was in this class for the first time. Our teacher, Mr. Eagle, placed him in one corner of the room, while indoctrinating him on the way the class works.

Today, our project was to draw a series of still-life images of pinecones, leaves, and other flowers. Our medium was charcoal pencils on white paper to do this. I took my time to do each one. I liked the picture of the flowers that I drew so well that I thought I would frame it and give it to my grandmother as a gift. She's getting up in years and enjoys whenever I draw things for her.

As class ended, Mr. Eagle instructed everyone to clean up their messes, and get to a stopping point if we were still working on something. When we accomplished that, everyone could get ready to go home or to any after-school activities we may be involved in. I would head to practice as soon as I leave here.

My liking of Elizabeth goes back a long way. Shortly after starting kindergarten, when I figured out that we were going to be in the same grade and seeing each other most every day, my crush on her began. This was long before I knew she would turn into the type of young woman she had. I could pick them early.

Back then, I would try to find time at the end of every day to speak to her a little bit. For a while, during kindergarten, I would ask her for a little harmless kiss at the end of every day. She would always laugh and tell me, "No."

However, I was undeterred. I kept asking.

On my sixth birthday, I repeated the same process I had done dozens of times before, but that time was different.

I asked Elizabeth to give me a kiss as a sixth birthday present, and with almost no hesitation, she gave me a sweet kiss right on the lips. It was fast. Only a peck. It was the first kiss I had ever had. Probably hers too.

I still smile when I think about that day. She probably doesn't even remember that kiss.

Coming back to the present, I took my opportunity at the end of this day to get a word in with Elizabeth while Arnie and Mary Jane were elsewhere. I wasn't looking for a kiss, but if she offered, I wouldn't say no.

I did not get to talk to her much during class today. We don't hang out during lunch or in the halls between classes, and since this was my only class besides the twenty-minute homeroom period at the beginning of the day, I don't see her as much as I would like. Getting face-to-face time with her at school is difficult. For her, this class isn't her favorite. She doesn't really have anyone here besides me she knows well.

"Hey, Elizabeth."

"Hi, Lucas," she said, looking up from her work.

"How has your day been?"

"Alright, I guess. I had a tough test in English class. I hope I passed."

"I'm sure you did," I said, as though I knew the results of the test before her. Thinking up a quick topic of conversation, I asked, "What do you think of the new kid?"

Her eyes shifted in his direction. "I don't know. He's all right."

She has just the sweetest voice, with just a bit of a southern drawl. I could listen to her talk all day.

"Yeah, I guess so," I said. "What are you going to be doing after school?"

"Well, I have cheerleading practice right after school. I think we're going to be practicing over next to the practice football field instead of in the gym."

I tried not to show it on my face, but this made my day. Although, it might distract me from my practice if I am busy watching her practice. I think I will live.

"Are you going to need a ride home after practice? I should have room," I said. I asked because she occasionally needs a lift back to her house if her family is too busy to get to her. She asked me before in advance. She would have known if she had a ride long before now, but it never hurts to take a shot.

Elizabeth smiled. "No, mom is going to pick me up today. How about we do it some other day?"

Nothing would please me more, I thought. I would never say it this way to her aloud, though. "That sounds nice. I guess that I'll be seeing you out by the practice field."

She nodded and smiled again. God, I love that smile. Even though we just talked for about five minutes, I still do not believe that she knows I am alive. Maybe I am just being too hard on myself.

The bell rang, and I was off to practice.

CHAPTER EIGHT

Tomorrow night was the annual game with our archrivals: The Richwood Lumberjacks. We are the only two high schools in our county separated by a mountain and the Cherry River.

There has been bad blood between our two schools ever since my dad played football here thirty years ago. It is normal for a few fights to break out during the game. It is also normal for the fights to break out in the stands as well. The police usually attend these games in full force. It's about the only time you can get away with speeding on Route 19. This year, the game is in Richwood.

We normally play each other on the Friday closest to Halloween. The bus for the visiting team will usually go back to its hometown covered in eggs, the jail gets full, and the odd street sign comes up missing. The blood has been running bad between the two towns for years, leading to some of the old timers getting into fights in the stands.

There is bad blood everywhere in our county.

During practice, Coach Nixon drilled the history of this rivalry between us, trying to get everyone pumped up about the game tomorrow. It's been working too. The assistant coaches have had to break up at least two fights so far in this practice.

Emotions were high. The coaches break up the fight, and Coach Nixon will tell the participants of the fight to save it for the Lumberjacks. They will see the logic in what he says, and that will usually calm them down.

I have been sharp in practice so far. I have completed almost every pass thrown. I'm pumped. The only passes that have fallen to the ground are those dropped by a receiver. A few times, receivers come back to the huddle shaking their stinging hands. Their hands hurt because I'm throwing too hard. They've asked me to tone it down a little, but that's not happening. Not today. Not tomorrow.

After all the hype that Coach Nixon heaped on me about Jake, about me being careful to make sure that he doesn't intercept any of my passes, he'd been quiet in practice. He got the chance to tip away one of my passes from the intended receiver. Other than that, I've barely noticed him on the field.

They put him in as the starter at free safety on defense. Someone must have given him a playbook to study before today. He's gotten all the reps in with the first-team defense so far.

I did not let the fact that Elizabeth and the entire cheerleading squad was over near the bleachers practicing their cheers for tomorrow night's game mess up my concentration. I was surprised. I love seeing Elizabeth dressed in her cheerleader uniform. For me, it is a good reason to get up in the morning. So, for me to be more focused on football than her is significant.

As I said, I'm locked in today.

Near the end of practice, the coach called for the first-team offense and the first-team defense to line up for a short, full contact scrimmage. This is rare that the day before a game.

Normally, we don't have a full-contact scrimmage the day before a game. Usually, the coaching staff takes it easy on us the day before a game. They don't want anybody to get hurt, but I know that there is a method to his madness.

We started on the twenty-yard line, with eighty yards of field in front of us. The play that Coach called for us to run on first down had two receivers on the left side of the line of scrimmage lined up together. They were going to go out about five yards and split. I had a third receiver split to the right. His assignment was to go long. He is my best receiver, so he had a corner playing him tight and a safety driving over from the defensive backfield. Jake lined up at safety, shadowing the two receivers split left.

I lined up behind the center and went through my cadence. The cadence is what a quarterback yells out before the center snapped the ball. It sounds like nonsense, but to those who know the plays, it makes perfect sense. Sometimes.

The center hiked the ball. I took it and dropped back five steps, surveying the field.

The two receivers lined up together, went out five yards and split, but their men blanketed them. I discarded them as options for the moment. The other receiver went long and the safety that shadowed towards him before the snap stuck with him in the corner who was already covering the receiver. It forced one of the three linebackers to cover the running back coming out of the backfield. The other two were locked up with the offensive line.

After reading the field and coverage, I decided there wasn't anyone on the defense accounting for me. I took off through a hole that opened on the right side of the line. I dodged by a linebacker who tried to grab me while still engaged with an offensive lineman, and then I planted a stiff-arm on one of the defensive backs.

Breaking free from the first level of the defense, I accelerated to my full speed. Am I the fastest guy? No, but I still can scramble effectively.

In no time, I was across the fifty-yard line. The back that was covering my good receiver broke coverage on him and hurried in my direction. He is fast, but not very strong. He bounced off me as he made contact, leaving only the strong safety with any chance to tackle me.

I crossed the thirty-yard line, the twenty, and then the ten.

As I barreled towards the end zone, there stood the strong safety, just waiting to meet me. I made a split-second decision that instead of trying to juke around him, I would try to plow right over him. I had the momentum on my side, and I figured that if it were to crash into him with me going at full speed and him standing stationary in front of the goal line, that I could easily push my way across the goal line with him in tow.

I came within five yards of the safety and the goal line, then out of the corner of my eye, I saw Jake hurtling towards me...

...And then nothing.

PART TWO

CHAPTER NINE

When Coach Dunlap left to take Lucas to the emergency room, he told all the players that practice was over. The mood in the locker room was somber as the guys showered and changed from their football uniforms.

Jake sat alone in one corner of the locker room. His teammates were giving him the silent treatment. From their point of view, Jake had just sent the starting quarterback—who was originally the backup quarterback—to the emergency room the day before the biggest game of the year. They did not have another quarterback because Lucas was the backup anyway, and Jake did not appear sorry or remorseful.

The mood in the locker room was somber, trending toward hostile. Everyone felt sorry for Lucas. They hoped he would be okay soon. As their thoughts moved past Lucas to the game against Richwood, they realized they didn't have a quarterback prepared to face their rivals, causing resentment to seethe from the other players towards the new guy.

Jake did not seem to notice any of this. He was in his own little world, tying his shoes, thinking about how long he would have to wait for his mom to get here to pick him up. He was pleased at how well he performed in practice. He thought that the couple of passes he broke up should have impressed everyone. He wondered why the tremendous hit that he put on Lucas didn't impress everyone. Everybody liked to see big hits at football games. For the life of him, he couldn't figure out why everyone was ignoring him. Maybe it was because nobody knew him yet.

"Oh, well," he thought. With his shoes now tied, he got up, slung his gym bag over his shoulder, and walked outside to wait for his mom to arrive.

He waited about ten minutes before his mother arrived in their minivan. His mom, Cherie, was in her early forties, and had a pleasant, motherly face. She was starting to put on some of the excess weight that a mother in her early forties puts on when she no longer has to work and stay at home all day, most days.

Jake got into the van, slung his gym bag back into the bench seat behind the front seats, and buckled his seat belt. His mom put the van in gear and pulled away.

"Hey, Jake," Cherie said pleasantly.

Jake stared at the dashboard. "Hey."

"So…how was your first day of school?"

Jake shrugged his shoulders. "All right, I guess."

Cherie saw that trying to draw her son into a conversation using indirect questioning would not work. She was not flustered. Someone had told her she might have to take a more direct approach in drawing her son into a detailed conversation.

So, using the tactic, she said, "Tell me about it."

"It was okay, I guess," Jake said. Cherie smiled to herself. "The teachers seem nice. I didn't talk to very many people. But I think I could learn to like this place."

"Good, good. How did your first practice go?"

Jake gave another shrug, but this time did not answer her question.

Concerned, Cherie looked over at him and saw that his hands were shaking. "Jake, what happened at practice?"

He sighed and looked out the window at the passing landscape of Summersville. "I thought it went pretty well. I made a couple of good plays, but nobody seemed to care."

"Oh. Why do you think that?"

"Because I think I broke the quarterback's shoulder."

Startled, Cherie almost jerked the van off the road. Jake still stared out the window as though nothing had happened. However, something had happened.

"How did you do that?" she asked in an even tone, trying not to sound upset.

"I tackled him."

"You just tackled him?"

"Yeah, it was a pretty hard hit, though. I couldn't help that he didn't see me coming."

"Did he do something to provoke you?" she asked, hoping that would not be the case.

"No," Jake responded. "He was just running up the field, and he was focused on getting around some other dude when I hit him. I think it knocked him out for a while. He was still woozy when the coach put him in his truck."

"Okay," Cherie said, heaving a sigh of relief.

She understood why nobody else cared about the rest of Jake's performance at practice. She hoped it would not become a proverbial black eye, haunting Jake.

Something suddenly popped into her head, "Jake, did you . . ."

"Yes mom. I did," Jake said, knowing where the question was going. "Right after I ate my cereal this morning."

Cherie let out a relieved breath. "Okay Jake, just checking. Good boy. We're having lasagna tonight. I thought that I'd make you your favorite dish to celebrate your first day of school."

Jake finally looked over at his mom and smiled. "Thanks mom," he said, and meant it.

Cherie thought that would do the trick.

CHAPTER TEN

Déjà vu. Sort of.

I was on the same beach with white sand flowing in both directions as far as the eye could see. Elizabeth was with me once again. This time, we sat beside each other on a blanket, sharing a picnic lunch. She smiled, and running her fingers through my hair and said, "Lucas, I cannot imagine being here with a better guy that you. I don't know why we didn't get together years ago."

I must have died because this must be heaven. Then she put her arm around my shoulder. This was nice. I wanted to melt into her embrace. Then she gripped me tighter, squeezing my shoulder harder than what I thought possible.

"Oww!" I yelled, and then suddenly I was lying in a strange bed and it was my mom who was running her fingers through my hair, not Elizabeth. She always seemed to be the spoiler of my dreams. Why did my shoulder hurt so darn much? I know I was not dreaming that.

"Oww!" I screamed again. Then I opened my eyes and looked around... a hospital room? "Where am I?" I tried to say, but it came out, "Wha mam ee?"

"You're here in the hospital baby," mom said softly at my side, "and you're on a lot of pain medication right now. So take it easy."

"What happened? What am I doing here? What is this pain in my shoulder?" I stammered out in quick succession.

"You were at football practice, when the new boy, Jake, I think they said his name was, tackled you and knocked you out and broke your right collarbone and gave you a concussion."

I moaned from both the news and the pain.

"You were unconscious for almost an hour. We were worried sick about you," she explained. "The doctor says that you can go home this afternoon, but you're going to have to have your arm in a sling for four weeks."

I let out another groan. There goes the Richwood game.

She continued, "However, the doctor gave orders to stay home for two weeks while your head heals. Apparently, you suffered a pretty severe concussion."

That was good news. A whole two weeks at home playing video games. I could deal with that. However, she had more bad news.

"Your teachers said that they will send home all your assignments with Allen, and that you can make them up at pretty much your own pace. You'll have to finish them by the time you go back to school, though."

There went my silver lining, I thought. I hated homework.

"After the doctor lets you take off your sling, you'll have to do a couple of weeks of rehabilitation to build the muscles in your arm back up."

I hated rehabilitation. I had to have it on a knee that I sprang while playing basketball during Junior High.

"Do you have any questions for me?"

"What happened to Jake?" I asked. The fog in my head began to lift. If I was this messed up, I could only imagine how the proverbial 'other guy' looked, since I was bigger than he was.

"Oh, he's fine," she answered. "He didn't get a scratch on him. Pretty lucky I guess."

This made me a little angry. I didn't know if it was because I got hurt and he didn't because of a hit he put on me, or if it was because I was embarrassed because of the way I thought it made me look.

"Let's get you out of that gown and get you into some regular clothes and get you home. Okay?"

I looked under the sheet for the first time to see myself dressed in a hospital gown that, I thought, looked a lot like a dress. I hoped no one saw me wearing this thing while I was knocked out. Now that would be embarrassing.

CHAPTER ELEVEN

It turned out that most of my friends saw me the evening I was in the hospital, gown and all. While I was off school, I did not hear the end.

"You looked so pretty in that dress, Lucas," was the statement I heard most often. Others included:

"That dress really brought out your eyes, Lucas."

"You'd make a cute girl, Lucas."

I couldn't remember which guy said that to me, but I found it kind of worrisome. Not for me, but it worried me about the guy who said it.

I heard it all over those two weeks. My brief vacation was not as enjoyable as I thought it would be. I could not play any sports, and I could barely play video games like I had hoped. I did not go anywhere. I went to the doctor twice for checkups. Although, I wouldn't consider that "going anywhere."

Allen brought my schoolwork every day. He brought no art homework home. He said Mr. Eagle had a project in store for me when I got back to school. I hoped his project would be easier than having to do a bunch of other projects that I had not seen demonstrated.

Most of the homework was easy, and I finished it a lot faster than I thought I would. I enjoyed the days during school when Blake would be at school, and therefore not bothering me. I saw most of my friends who lived near me about every day. I even got a lot of mail, which was exciting for me. Most of it was 'Get Well Soon' cards from people that my parents knew, relatives, people from my church, my class, and one or two teachers.

I got a lot of presents from my parents and my grandparents. I got a couple of video games, some new shoes, and the best: money. Since I did not get to go anywhere, I didn't get to spend any of it. Like all seventeen-year-olds, money burns a hole in my pocket if I have some for longer than twenty minutes.

So went my doctor-imposed vacation. Tomorrow, it will be time to go back to school. I had only seen Jake once since I got home from the hospital. His parents brought him over to my house the day after I got home from the hospital to see how I was doing, and to apologize. The apology seemed to be forced. I have not seen or heard from him since then.

Elizabeth called me once during my time at home to see how I was doing. She was there when I took the hit from Jake and felt so bad when it happened. I felt my heart race after her call, hoping that she would call me back. She didn't.

Ashley came to see me and visit about every other day. Most times when she came, she would bring me little snacks or candy, or just anything to cheer me up. She would not stay for very long, just long enough to see how I was doing. It was nice to know that someone from school cared that much about me.

I had heard from my classmates that Jake was fitting in fine with everybody. Stone was the only one who did not seem to get along well with him. I think that was because he was holding a grudge against Jake for the hit that he put on me. That is why he is my best friend.

I even heard that Jake and Elizabeth seemed to get along well in my absence. I have known Elizabeth for a long time, and I know she will talk to any guy that's even halfway attractive. I know there was nothing I can do to stop her from talking to other guys, but I wished she would pay the same attention to me sometimes.

CHAPTER TWELVE

Jake had been busy over the past couple of weeks. He was getting well acclimated to his new surroundings but was having a bit of a hard time making friends. He was making some inroads, though. His mom and dad seemed to be happy now that he was staying out of trouble at school. He was even getting good grades for the first time in some years.

He was preparing to go to bed when his dad came to his room and stood in the doorway. His dad was a big man in his late thirties. His hair and beard saw some salt and pepper sneak in. He had hands that could be best described as 'meat hooks' and what was once a well-trimmed body showed some mileage. He had an intelligent, calm demeanor that allowed him to progress rapidly up the career ladder to the position that he had in his company through a mix of swift decision-making and a level of unmatched dedication to his job. His superiors took notice and promotions came rapidly.

His dad was unnaturally calm in his dealings with Jake. Jake was about like any other teenage boy. He got into trouble sometimes. However, Jake's past problems were of the monumental variety. Very public.

During those times, his dad had never raised his voice, nor did anything to harm him. He did not even so much as spank him when he was younger. *Ever.* To save the family from humiliation, he just applied for a transfer at his job, packed up the family, and moved. *Three times.*

"Jake," he said in a deep voice, leaning against the doorframe, "I've heard it through the grapevine that Lucas is returning to school tomorrow. There's not going to be any trouble between you two, is there?"

"Not that I know of dad. I'd only known him for that one day when 'it' happened." There was no need to describe what had happened aloud. It was a touchy subject in the Schofield household. "I sure don't have a problem with him. He seemed like a nice guy. I felt bad about it," Jake said as he unmade his bed.

"I know you did," his dad said, crossing his arms. "It's just that your mom and I like this town and we would like to stay here, okay?"

"Okay dad."

"Have you…," he started to ask.

"Yes, sir," Jake cut him off.

"Good. Now you get some sleep. I'll see you in the morning."

"Good night dad. I love you." Jake reached over to his nightstand and turned off the light.

That almost brought a tear to the big guy's eye. His son had not said that to him in years. He could not think of the last time that he had said that. It almost made him suspicious, as if Jake would have to have ulterior motives for saying something like that.

Jake went to sleep on Sunday night at home feeling almost as anxious as he did before his first night of school here. Tomorrow, Lucas would be returning to school. Jake had been reluctant to speak with him since that first day of school. He hoped Lucas would not be too mad when he returned to school.

CHAPTER THIRTEEN

When I awoke for school the next morning, I struggled to put my clothes on. I never realized how hard it would be to put on shirts and pants with only one arm. I am sure that I had to have been funny to watch. My shoulder seemed to heal just fine, but it sometimes still hurt like crazy.

I was happy to be returning to school. If you were to tell any kid that they could stay home from school for two weeks, I would bet that the majority would jump at the chance. I would have too, but I never realized how much of a big part school was in my life.

Other than the ones who came to visit, I missed my friends. I missed going to the gym and playing ball with my friends. I missed football practice and games. Our season is ending this upcoming Friday with a game against Oak Hill, but at least I could watch from the sidelines if I wanted to. Then two weeks after that, basketball practice starts. I hope my shoulder feels well enough so that I can try out for the Varsity team and not the Junior Varsity team like Coach Nixon had told me about. I just hoped I would be healthy enough to try out at all.

Going out to my car to find my brother and my friends out there already waiting for me felt good. I had my lunch in one hand, and mom had made Blake carry my book-bag for me. It embarrassed him to do it. It only made matters worse when everybody standing around started taking verbal jabs at him.

"Hey Lucas," Brian said. "I know they gave you some pills and your sling when you got out of the hospital, but I didn't know that they give out trained monkeys as well."

"Shut up," Blake said to Brian. "I'm not his monkey. I can't help it if he's too weak to carry this thing," he said, hoisting the backpack.

"I'm not too weak to carry it ya' moron," I said to him. "I only have one arm right now and can't carry everything." I had to place my lunch down on top of the car so I could get my keys out to unlock it.

"Well, why don't you just put your lunch in here and that way you'll have your arm free?" Blake said, trying to find a way out of his task.

"There's no room for my lunch in there. It's holding all of my books." I opened the door, reached up, and grabbed my lunch.

"So that's why it's so heavy," he said, as if it were a revelation to everyone. He was carrying it, so he should have some idea of what was in it.

I rolled my eyes.

It was not worth wasting my breath on. "So, how are you going to practice with that sling around your arm?" he asked.

"Well, I'm not," I said. "The doctor said no playing sports until he says so. I may not even be able to play basketball this year."

"Yeah, but you broke your right shoulder. You're left-handed. Can you play anything? It's not like you used it, anyway."

"I use it to help me catch things. I use it to help balance me as I throw the football, and kind of as a guide. When I'm running, it bounces up and down. I imagine that would probably hurt right now," I said.

Sometimes Allen's elevator does not go all the way to the top, if you know what I mean.

Usually, they would tell me I was just making excuses, trying to get out of playing. I had an obvious excuse so as not to do my normal things, and no one could really claim that I was faking it. "C'mon, get in the car. We're running late." As usual.

We picked up Stone and continued to school. I found that driving my car was not as difficult as I thought it would be. I used my left hand to steer the car, anyway. Brian was in his usual shotgun seat this morning. He helped me to shift the gears, tune the radio, and handle the heater. The car was automatic, so there was not very much shifting of gears.

As usual, we made to school just as the bell rang, which was also about the time that Mrs. Gibson ran through the door. Most teachers get to school an hour before the classes start. That way, they can look over their lesson plans, maybe eat a little breakfast, or just relax a little before the craziness of the school day ensues.

Not Mrs. Gibson, though. For whatever reason, she does not relish the quiet before the storm. Instead, she likes to arrive at the tumultuous time that the storm begins.

I took my usual seat behind Stone and in front of Allen. Mrs. Gibson took the roll call.

When she got to my name, I said, "Here."

She said, "It's good to have you back, Mr. Caine."

I was as much of a reception as I should have expected.

After she took the roll and went to look over her notes on whatever she was going to be teaching today, Jake sauntered over to where we were sitting. "Hey fellas," he said.

"Hey," Stone, Allen and I said in unison.

"How's it going?" Stone asked. Allen and I remained silent.

"Fine, I guess," he replied, then turned to me. "It's good to have you back. I'm sorry again about what happened. I really hated to begin my time here with something like that happening. I'm also sorry that I haven't been down to check and see how you were doing after that first time I came down. I was afraid that you might hate me or something."

"Naw man," I said, brushing the issue aside with the wave of my hand, "it was just an accident. I understand. It's part of the game. Don't worry about it."

He breathed a sigh of relief. "I'm glad. I didn't want to make any enemies here in my first month."

"What? You have enemies somewhere else?" Stone asked jokingly.

"There are some kids that I've moved away from that didn't like me too well when I left," he said in all seriousness.

"Oh, I was just kidding," Stone said.

Jake looked at Stone. "Oh. Okay," he said, and then turned and walked back to his seat.

There was something a little off about the way he said that. Suspicious.

I looked at Stone when Jake left and whispered, "What was that all about?"

He shrugged his shoulders in an 'I don't know' gesture. I turned around. Allen had a confused look on his face.

I watched Jake walk back to his seat and used this as an excuse to look at Elizabeth as he passed her. She had her wavy, blonde hair pulled back into a ponytail, and was wearing a navy blue 'Ron-Jon's Surf Shop' t-shirt. My heart raced from seeing her for the first time in two weeks.

We spent the rest of the study period without saying much to each other. I wondered what Jake's story was. I had learned that he had been to several schools because his dad had some kind of government job or something and that he had to move around a lot.

The conversation we just had left a few questions. He said he had enemies in places he lived before. That said that he left on bad terms with someone or some people. What did he do for that to happen, at least twice? It baffled me.

I looked over to see Jake and Elizabeth engaged in a hushed conversation. I could only guess what it was about, but judging by Elizabeth's body language, I would say that our boy Jake was trying to do some flirting with her. Judging from how she was responding to him, I would say that Jake's attempts were proving to be quite unsuccessful.

I thought it was funny.

CHAPTER FOURTEEN

In the gym class where I was the teacher's aide, I could not really do much. I just sat in the bleachers and went over my biology homework. I was afraid that since I had missed the last two weeks, that I would be so far behind everybody else that it would take me a couple of days to get back into the flow of things.

This got a few scowls from Coach Nixon, because even though I could not play for the rest of the football season, he thinks I should be in his office, going over game film preparing for next year.

I looked up at one point to watch the game of basketball that the guys were playing. They are playing five-on-five, full court. One team has its shirts on; the other team is not wearing shirts. When two teams play like this, they call it 'Shirts versus Skins."

About half of these guys that are playing on the court right now don't usually play any basketball except for when they're made to in gym class. This left maybe four or five guys on the entire court who know what they're doing.

As I watched the game unfold, I realized the person controlling the game for his team was Jake. He was on the Skins team, and the one tasked with bringing the ball up the court. He seemed to run his inexperienced team well on both ends of the court. I saw him make two very long three-pointers on consecutive trips down the court.

If I had just done that, I would have been whooping and hollering, and everyone in the gym would have known that I had just sunk two consecutive bombs. Jake barely even cracked a smile during the entire process. Odd. Either he was very focused on the game, or something was wrong with him.

With my attention on the game, I failed to notice that there was now someone sitting next to me. It was Ashley. She's pretty, but not in a classic way. I don't know how to describe it. She's cute in her own way.

"Hey Lucas," she said, leaning over and bumping my good shoulder.

"Hey Ash," I said. Today, she wore a pair of nice, little blue jogging shorts with a gold tank top. She had her hair tied back in a ponytail, leaving her ears exposed to the world. I know it sounds weird, but I always thought Ashley had cute ears. Somehow, I found that when she had her hair tied back or put up and I could see her ears, that she was a lot more attractive.

While I was out recovering from my injury, my friends would drop by and see how I was doing for a few minutes or give me a courtesy call occasionally. Ashley came over to my house almost every day to visit. I really found it sweet that she did that for me. She provided good company for me when most friends were in a hurry to leave and go play video games or whatever.

Ashley and I had been good friends for as long as I can remember. She is the only friend that I have that I know I can rely on if I were to find myself in a pinch. Even Stone sometimes does not return my calls. I expressed my thanks to her for spending time with me over these past couple of weeks.

"Aww, it was nothing," she said with a wave of her hand. "I thought that if I were in that situation that you would do the same for me."

"Well, I really appreciate it," I said, giving her a brief hug. Personally, I don't know if I would have done the same for her, but when she put it that way, it made me think. After a moment of silence, I asked, "How's it going?"

"That's what I was going to ask you," she replied. "I still can't get over what happened to you. Had I been there, I would have kicked him in the shins."

"Who?"

"Jake, that's who, that seems kind of mean to be celebrating and dancing around someone who is lying still on the ground from something that you've done to him, so I would have kicked him for celebrating about what he did."

"Thanks. I'm glad that someone would have had my back."

She smiled, "Lucas, we've known each other since I can remember, and I don't enjoy seeing anything bad happen to you, just the same as you wouldn't like to see any harm come to me."

I smiled back, "That's what friends are for, right?"

"So how are you doing?" she finally got down to asking. "Is your shoulder doing, okay?"

"I guess it is. It hurts like hell sometimes. But I guess that I'm doing okay." I involuntarily grasped my shoulder as if to show my point.

"That's good," she responded, ending the subject of my shoulder. She knows I am not going to complain about it, so there is nothing much to talk about. She switched subjects. "Has Jake apologized to you?"

"Yeah"

"Do you forgive him?"

I looked over to where he was on the gym floor, closely guarding the guy with the ball.

"I guess I do," I shrugged. She didn't look convinced. "I mean, what's to forgive? I got injured during practice. I know I risk getting hurt like that every time that I put on pads."

"Oh," she said like she understood. "No sense in harboring a grudge against someone you barely know. So, are you two going to be friends?"

"I don't know. I guess so."

"It sounds to me like you're doing some guessing." Ashley is one of the smartest girls in the class, so it is no surprise to me she noticed this. What surprised me was that she was right. I *was* doing some guessing.

"You're right Ashley. I hadn't thought of it that way. It's either that I don't know him well enough yet, or he seems kind of strange to me. But maybe I just haven't been around him as much as everyone else."

To my surprise, she said, "I think he's kind of strange."

"What?" I asked if as though she read my mind.

"I think he's kind of strange," she repeated. "There are times he seems normal, and then sometimes he acts very odd. It's just strange. I don't like him sitting over on my side of the room during home room. He gives me the creeps sometimes when he's talking to Liz."

"Why?"

"Sometimes, all he seems to want to do is flirt with Liz or me or any other girl that he can get to talk to him. Those are the days he wants to talk. Some days, he doesn't say much at all. Then there are some days where he acts kind of weird, then there are days where he's acting normal, but he's really irritable."

"Most guys will talk to any girl that will talk to them." I explained, letting her in a little guy secret. "How do you mean 'irritable'?"

"You know how the kids are in this school. If they find an opening, they'll pick on you over any little thing."

"Oh yeah," I agreed. "Try walking around here for a day with a sling around your shoulder. Talk about no mercy."

She laughed. "Well, there are days where I will see people pick on him like we would any other guy, and he doesn't seem to care. Those are the days when he is acting kind of weird. But on the days, he'll get mad, and say bad things to us when we pick on him."

"What kind of bad things?" I asked, watching Jake guard someone on the court.

"He calls us some terrible names. I even heard him threaten to smack a girl if she didn't leave him alone."

I shook my head. "That's horrible. Guys shouldn't talk to girls that way. Nobody should talk to anyone like that for any reason."

"You're the only boy that I've gone to school with that never treated us girls like we have cooties. You've never treated our ideas and opinions in class like they're coming from 'stupid little girls,'" she said, resting her hand on my arm. The display of intimacy came as a bit of a surprise. She does this now and then, but I'm still never prepared for it.

When I thought about what she just said, she had a point. I never thought that the girls in our class differed greatly from us boys and I treat them that way. Ashley was the only girl over the years that I felt easy talking with. I don't know why. There is just this comfort level between the two of us that has formed over the years. Why was it so hard for me to talk to other girls sometimes? I could write another book on that subject.

"Thanks," I said. I don't know how to handle comments like that from people, so I just say 'thanks' and move on with it.

"So, have you talked any to Elizabeth?" she asked, switching subjects again. Ashley has known about my crush on Elizabeth for years. Even though she is best of friends with Elizabeth, she never told her about my crush on her. I do not know why. I thought girls tell each other *everything*.

"Not much," I said. "She told me this morning that she's happy to have me back. That's about all."

I suddenly heard Coach Nixon blow his whistle. The boys that were the skins team were putting their shirts back on. I looked over at Ashley and say, "It looks like gym is over."

She followed my gaze and said, "Looks like it."

"I guess that I'll talk to you later." She stood up, sliding her hand down my arm to my hand, and pulled me up after her.

She gave me a quick hug and walked away.

CHAPTER FIFTEEN

Lunchtime. The gross pizza was on the menu again. It was raining outside, so every kid was inside the cafeteria to eat. Some kids go outside to eat this time of year. Now that it is getting closer to winter, and it is getting colder. With the chilly rain coming down outside, many of the kids that usually go outside to eat during the pleasant months are all inside the cafeteria, which makes it much more crowded.

I sat in my usual spot beside Allen at the lunch table. Stone's spot was vacant. He was sitting next to some girl a grade ahead of us at another table. Typical Stone. Eric and another guy named William sat across from me. Jake sat in between William and Ben, who is a cousin of mine.

Ben is a relative of mine that had a rough childhood. His dad used to beat him and his wife up before he walked out on them when Ben was about seven years old. Now his mom sometimes has a job, and sometimes she does not, but she neglects Ben no matter what she is doing. About three or four years ago, Ben stopped talking to people, stopped doing his homework. He cut himself off from everybody. His mom did not seem to care.

Our elementary school teacher then, Mrs. Boyd, cared. She noticed all of this going on with Ben and told our principal. The principal had Ben looked at by a child psychologist during school time without telling Ben's mom. There was probably something illegal about that, but it was the only way Ben was going to get any help.

I do not know what went on during their meeting, but a couple of weeks after the meeting, Ben started talking more and more. He started doing his homework again. He seemed much better, except for one thing.

He did not get excited about anything . . . ever, and Ben was one of the most animated kids I knew until that point. He had all kinds of funny screeches or noises that he was constantly making. He no longer made any crazy sounds.

When he would get a good grade on a test, he would act as though it was nothing special, even though we all knew Ben rarely ever got good grades on anything. When we were in elementary school, we often played kickball at recess. Occasionally Ben would kick a home run during these games, and he would jog around the bases, touch home plate, and then sit down. He did not smile, give high fives, or do anything. We all thought that was weird.

What had happened was after he met with the psychologist, the psychologist declared Ben to be clinically depressed. Then he put Ben on some pills. These pills made him associate with everyone again, but it was not the same Ben. It turned him into the Ben that we have been around for the last several years, a quieter Ben. We accept this, and we treat Ben the same way that we always had before. All his friends are happy that he does not seem to be depressed any more.

Eating with only one arm is a difficult thing to do. It was hard to open the plastic packaging on one of my snack cakes, or twist off the cap on my drinks. Nobody seemed too inclined to help me out, so I had to suffer through lunch like this. This was probably how it was going to be for the next couple of weeks.

The conversation seemed to flow as it usually did. Everybody was talking about what happened over the weekend. The guys were picking on me a little about my struggles with my lunch. Everyone was picking on Allen about something or other.

"Hey man! Leave me alone!" Allen shouted to Ricky at one point.

"Aww, the poor baby, He can't take it when someone picks on him," Ricky said as if he were talking to a little girl.

"I can too!" Allen protested.

"Whatever." Some of the other kids from around the table said at about the same time. Allen got so mad that he lowered his head and ate his lunch silently; his cheeks flushed red the entire time.

"Hey big boy," Ricky said, finding another target to pick on: me. He was the other 'big boy' in my grade. He's not very tall, but built like a tank. Some considered him the class bully, but if you really knew him, he was as kind as a cow. "What did you do during gym class? Play with all the little girls since you couldn't play with the boys?"

"No," I replied, and then muttered "pervert" under my breath.

"Don't you have a dress that you could wear to play with them?"

Everybody around the table broke out with laughter. No one was going to let me forget my hospital gown. I knew that the jokes about it were forthcoming, and I imagine Ricky had spent a week coming up with that joke. I thought that silence was the best answer, so I remained quiet.

As lunch went on, I watched Jake as he sat next to Ben. I noticed they behaved the same way, except that Jake spoke a little more than Ben did. That was still quiet compared to everyone else.

That struck me as odd. Nobody acted like Ben, unless...

I left the thought unfinished in my head. I did not want to go down that road. Jake was new, and I would not pass complete judgment on him. Yet. You can't judge a book by its cover until you dig into it.

After I finished my lunch, I sat around shooting the breeze with the guys. These were the times I enjoyed the most at school. The camaraderie existing between my classmates and me. Some of whom I have known my entire life. I have always been told to savor the time that I had in school now because once we graduate and get out into the real world, times like these come few and far in between.

Ashley got up and came over from where she was sitting with Elizabeth and sat down in Stone's empty seat.

"You should go talk to her," she said.

"Who?"

"Elizabeth. We were just talking about you, and she seemed a little sad that she hadn't spoken to you more since you broke your shoulder. I thought maybe since you two hadn't had the chance to really speak to each other that you could take the initiative and go over there." She said all of this in my ear so none of the other guys could hear what the conversation. I am glad they were so engrossed in their conversations so as not to eavesdrop on ours.

"I can't," I said, as though it would be illegal for me to do this.

"Why not? She's just sitting there all by herself. Just go over there and talk to her."

I looked over at Elizabeth sitting about halfway across the Commons Area. Ashley was right. She seemed to be alone.

"I don't know," I said tentatively.

"Look Lucas, you've liked her for a long, long time. Right?"

I nodded dumbly.

She continued, "If you don't start talking to her soon, nothing is ever going to happen between the two of you. We're going to be out of school before you know it. I know you Lucas, and I know that if you don't do anything, that you'll be kicking yourself for years."

I knew what she was saying. I am just shy about talking to Elizabeth. That is why I enjoy sitting next to her in art class so much. I do not have to step out of my comfort zone with her.

"Will you go over there with me?"

She rolled her eyes. "Good lord. If you want me to. Come on, let's go talk to her."

I looked at her, smiled tightly, and then nodded my head. "Okay, let's go."

"You lead the way."

I got up, walked over to where Elizabeth was sitting, and sat down beside her, careful not to bump my shoulder. She looked up from her lunch and smiled. Oh, how I love that smile.

"Hi," I said.

"Hey, Lucas," she said, the smile still on her face. She seemed happy to see me. "How are you doing?"

"I've heard that question about a million times today. I'm doing all right considering that I'm the one-armed man," I said, drawing a laugh from her. "How are you doing? I've only got to ask Ashley that question," I said jerking my thumb beside me to where Ashley was supposed to be sitting.

I looked over to find Ashley waving at me from where we were sitting to begin with, beside Allen. That little sneak let me go by myself. I just smiled and shook my head at her. She knew I was going to say something to her later about betraying me like this.

"Oh, I'm doing fine, I suppose," Elizabeth said. I found that talking with her was not as hard as I thought it would be. My hands were steady, at least. Maybe I did not need any support after all. "I've missed you not being here. I've missed you in art class."

My heart skipped a beat. I did not know what to say to this, other than, "I've missed not being there."

She smiled. "It's like summer. You don't know how much you miss it until it's gone," she said, causing my heart to skip another beat.

She smelled good today; her perfume reminded me of the summer. She seemed to smell good every day. I kept this comment to myself.

"I always looked forward to talking to you during art class, but when you weren't here, I missed it."

With me being tongue-tied as I am around girls, I did not know how to approach this or what to say. I just said, "Me too."

We sat in silence for a few minutes while she finished her lunch. Suddenly she leaned over and confided in a low voice, "I dropped off of the cheerleading squad this morning. Nobody knows about it yet."

This was an enormous shock to me. As I have mentioned before, Elizabeth has been a cheerleader ever since she was old enough to hold pom-poms.

"Why did you do that? I thought you loved being a cheerleader?"

"I used to," she said, still maintaining eye contact. "I just got bored with it. I hated having to go to practice every night. I hated going to all the football games and standing out in the cold with just a thin layer of spandex covering my legs. With the start of basketball season coming up, having to go cheer at twenty games—and put in the practice—just seemed like too much to me. You know what I'm saying?"

"Well, when you put it that way, I don't think that I'd want to do all of that," I sympathized.

"At least one person understands me," she said, returning her attention to the basketball game. "Every person who I've told that to, or has found out about it, thinks that I'm nuts."

"I don't think that you're nuts," I told her, still trying to hold on to that eye contact. "To be honest, I had been thinking that after this year, I was only going to play one sport. Basketball or football. With me breaking my collarbone, I am probably not going to be playing basketball anyway this year with tryouts already over. It just gets to be too much. I don't have enough time to focus in on all my homework or spend time with my family and friends."

"Exactly! That's almost exactly how I feel!" she said, giving me a hug. She released the hug, but grabbed my hand. The people sitting around us looked up from their meals to stare at us. She apologized.

After getting to know Elizabeth, I know that she secretly craves attention. Maybe she is getting a little tired of cheerleading. She can still do things around the school to get attention.

"Lucas, at least you know what I go through, and don't think of these extracurricular activities as being part of a popularity contest. So far, you're the only person who I've talked to that thinks along the same lines as me."

"I don't particularly like being in the limelight all that much myself. I'd rather stay under the radar than attract too much attention."

I sometimes wish that the senior quarterback had not have broken his arm and thrust me into the starting quarterback position. That is until I broke my shoulder. I enjoyed playing quarterback, but it never occurred to me how much attention the quarterback gets from the faculty and even the local newspaper. Seemingly, after every game, the local sports reporter would come up to me and want me to give a statement about how my team performed in the game if we won, or how I underperformed in the game if we lost. It is always the quarterback's fault if the team loses.

Not wanting the focus to be on me, I asked, "How have you been these past couple of weeks?"

She sighed. Let out a breath. "Do you know Eric's college roommate, Andrew? He is the guy that he brought home with him over the summer for a few weeks."

I know all about what happened to Andrew. I know when Eric brought Andrew to their house for the first time that Elizabeth instantly developed a huge crush on him. I did not know if it was because he was good looking, because he was a college guy, or a combination of the two. Whatever it was, Elizabeth had it big for him. I met him once, and I did not see what Elizabeth saw in him.

I could be biased.

Apparently, Andrew felt about the same way about Elizabeth that she did for him. Except, he was nearly nineteen and Elizabeth was only fifteen. Her parents did not allow them to do too much together, but I know from Ashley that they got close over the summer.

"I think I remember him."

"Well, I don't know if you ever found out, but Andrew and I had a relationship going over the summer." I nodded. She continued, "When he left, I thought everything was great. When he came back, he dumped me. He said that he had hooked up with some incoming freshman chick."

I wanted to laugh and ask her what she expected when she hooked up with a college guy.

"I'm sorry," I said instead.

She made a pouty face for just a second. "I guess that it's time to find someone my age. What do you think?"

That sounds like a great idea, I thought to myself, but respond more coolly, "Maybe someone closer to your own age might be for the best for right now."

"That's what I was thinking," she said cryptically. I did not know what she was thinking, but I knew that smile. She gives that smile when she is scheming something. I hoped that since she was telling me this, that I might finally be a part of that grand scheme.

I looked at the clock on the wall and noted that lunchtime was almost over. I looked down at her empty tray and offered to empty it for her.

I think I scored a brownie point there, asking to empty her tray even though I only have the one arm.

"Thanks, Lucas, that would be nice of you," she said.

"Okay, well, I'll see you this afternoon," I said that as she released my hand. I stood and picked up her tray with my good arm.

"I'm looking forward to it," she said with a mischievous grin on her face.

God, she is cute.

CHAPTER SIXTEEN

After what seemed like the longest biology class of my life, in which Coach Wheeler constantly referred to me as 'Lucas *Caine* I Get Some Drugs for My Shoulder', I was back in my favorite class.

Mr. Eagle pulled me aside at the beginning of class, and told me that in my time off, that the class had done about ten different projects. He said that he did not expect me to do all ten of them, and that was why he never had Allen bring any work home to me. He said to make up for all ten of them, he wanted me to get a sheet of white poster board and re-create any of the French Impressionist paintings only using various shades of charcoal pencils.

"Do you think that you could have that for me by next Monday?" he asked.

"Yeah, I suppose I could," I answered. "You're sure not going to make this easy on me, are you?"

He laughed. "Well, Lucas, I think you can handle this one project, or would you rather have all ten of the ones we that we did while you were gone to do by next week?"

"I'll do the re-creation in that case."

He chuckled again. "I figured that you'd see it my way. Have fun with it. If you do as well as I figure you will, I'll see that we hang it in the hall, or possibly use it as the cover of this year's yearbook. How does that sound?"

"That sounds great, though it adds some pressure."

"I never said that it was going to be easy. No, go sit down."

I gave a mock military salute with my good arm. "Yes sir!"

I was surprised when I sat down to find that the seating arrangement had changed in my time away from school. In my absence, Arnie and Mary Jane became a couple. Apparently. They now sat beside each other on one side of the table, which left me sitting beside Elizabeth.

A lot can happen in two weeks.

I had a heart attack when I sat down. Without a word, Elizabeth reached over, squeezed my hand, and smiled at me. "I'm glad you're back. If I have to listen to these two," she gestured at Arnie and Mary Jane, who were listening to our conversation with a little interest, "gush over each other anymore, I'm going to go crazy."

"Hey now!" Arnie said with long, scraggily hair falling in his eyes, putting his arm around Mary Jane. "Leave me and my baby out of this."

"Your baby?" I asked, thinking that never in a million years would I see this happening. "When did this happen?"

"We saw each other at the movie theater one night; we were both going to go watch the same movie," Mary Jane said. "We were both by ourselves, so we went in to the movie and sat together. He did the old 'yawn and put your arm around the girl' tactic. I didn't make him move his arm and by the end of the movie Arnie had his tongue down my throat." She shrugged. "It was just one of those things."

"Hey, you didn't seem to mind too much." Arnie said.

They continued to bicker with each other as I tuned their conversation out. I have known Arnie and Mary Jane for a few years, and I would have never pictured these two ever getting together. Everyone knows that both Arnie and Mary Jane are hotheads. I know little about relationships, but I know that when you throw two hotheads together in a relationship, you could possibly start a fire. Around here, that could be a literal fire. I would like to see if this relationship lasted a month.

As Mr. Eagle started in on his lesson, I noticed that Elizabeth still had a hold of my hand. I did not know what to make of this. Was Elizabeth just being affectionate, or was she showing me her feelings towards me? Whatever it was, I was enjoying it.

What Mr. Eagle was having us do today was to make a two-perspective drawing of a city using a ruler. We could make our city in any style we wanted to. We just had to make sure that I directed all lines at one of the perspective points on either side of the sheet of paper, and that we had at least ten discernable buildings in our city. I decided I was going to model my little city after the New York City skyline pre -9/11. That way, everyone would know immediately what city it was that I was drawing.

Elizabeth was having a little trouble figuring out just what lines were to go to which perspective point. She asked me if I could help her. "Do you remember when we had to do the city with just the one perspective?" I asked. She nodded. "Well, in that one, all the lines that were going away from you did what?"

"They all went to the little dot in the middle."

"Right, and all the vertical lines went straight up and down. The vertical lines here on what we're doing are still going to do that. On the other one, the horizontal lines that were on the front of the buildings didn't slope to the perspective point. Well, with what we're doing today, if a line is not a vertical line, then it's going to slope towards one of the perspective points on one side of the page. Do you understand?"

"Yeah," she smiled. "Thanks."

"Ok." I could not help but return the smile. "Watch me for a minute and see if you can figure it out." I quickly sketched out six lines and formed a simple building. "See, it's not that hard, is it? Think you can try it?"

"Yeah, I think I can do that," she said. She traced out six lines and made a decent outline of a building. "Like that?"

"I think that you're getting the hang of it. Now put a door or two and some windows and then you'll be well on your way to having a nice-looking building."

"Thanks Lucas. What would I do if you weren't here?" she asked rhetorically. We were quiet for a while, while we both became engrossed in our drawings. A little while later, she asked me, "How does it look so far?"

I looked over at her paper and saw that she had an almost realistic city started. "Pretty good."

She leaned over to see what I was drawing. "Is that New York?" I nodded. "Wow. That's superb, Lucas."

"Thanks."

"Look, Lucas, I'm not getting very far on my city so far. What are you doing after school?" Elizabeth said, asking me the question that I had been waiting for her to ask me since I've known her.

"Well, I can't do much. About all that I can do is play video games and do my homework. Why?" *Please, please let her ask that I wanted her to ask*, I thought to myself.

"I was wondering if maybe you could drive me home and we could work on my drawing. What do you say?"

Yes! I thought to myself with an exclamation point. However, I replied with a much cooler, "Yeah, we could do that. The other guys I bring to school every morning will be at football practice, but I think that they're going to find another ride home after practice since I'm not going to be there. I think that we could do that, yeah."

My mind was floating in the clouds now. She would quickly bring me back down to earth.

"Great, now that I don't have cheerleading practice, I have time for homework. I'll make us some pizza, and maybe, if she wants, and you're okay with it, we could invite Ashley over too," she said, biting her lip.

How could I say "no" to her when she bites her lip? This would ruin a nice evening alone with Elizabeth, but any time spent with her is worth it. Maybe if Ashley were there, she might keep me from saying something stupid and making a fool of myself.

"Sure," I replied. "Do you want me to go ask her if she wants to come? I think that I'm at a stopping point with my drawing."

I got up, walked across the room, and kneeled behind Ashley.

"What's going on?" she asked, poking me in the ribs playfully. "I see you've been over there talking to Elizabeth the entire period, almost. Hmm. Something brewing between you two?"

"Oww!" I grabbed my ribcage where her finger went perfectly in between two ribs. "I don't know. What happened to at lunch, by the way?"

"I just thought that you could handle it on your own," she explained. "It looks like you did alright to me. I saw her give you a hug and hold your hand."

It seemed to me as though she had a frown on her face when she said this, but I did not ask why.

"She also grabbed my hand at the beginning of this class and held it for a while, saying again that she was happy that I was back. Then she asked if I would take her home this evening and help her work on her perspective drawing."

"Ooo, you dog! Why aren't you more excited?" she asked when she saw the look on my face.

"She wanted me to come over here and ask you if you want to come with us. I didn't want to, but I wanted to make her happy. So, I came. Do you want to come?"

"Yeah," she said. "But I don't want to ruin any plans that you might have. Just tell her I can't."

"Maybe it might be better if you come, that way, if it gets too awkward, you can step in and help me out."

"That sounds like it might be for the best. We both know how you like to stick your foot in your mouth around girls," she laughed. "But I'll come only if you're sure you don't mind."

"That's true," I agreed. "She told me she's going to make us some pizza, so if nothing else productive comes out of our evening, at least we'll get some of that."

"Sounds like a plan."

***

When school ended, I made it out to my car before either Ashley or Elizabeth arrived. I was standing up against the car when the first of the football players on the team started coming out of the side door of the gym and started leisurely making their way towards the practice field. My car was parked near the double doors on the side of the gym. A couple of the guys teased me, asking why I wasn't going to practice. I shrugged them off. I knew that in their hearts that they all still loved me.

I looked to my right to see that Elizabeth and Ashley had just come out of the double doors coming from the cafeteria. I could not take my eyes off Elizabeth. She had on a black overcoat over a pair of tight jeans that left little to the imagination.

I asked Elizabeth if she wanted to ride up front with me. She got in the front seat, and Ashley walked around to the side where I was standing. She was looking cute today herself. She reached up and rubbed the corner of my mouth with a finger.

"Just wiping the drool off," she said.

Was it that obvious? I asked myself.

"Ha, ha," I opened her door and closed it behind her after she settled into the back seat. I got in the car, started the ignition, and put the car in reverse.

I looked out the windshield and saw Jake standing not ten feet away from the front of my car. He seemed to stare figurative laser beams at me and Elizabeth sitting together in the car. I looked over at Elizabeth, but she was busy looking into the back seat and talking to Ashley. She apparently did not see Jake at all.

What was that all about?

As I pulled onto Route 19 and away from the school, I could not help but thinking more about the scene with Jake than about finally having a 'study date' with Elizabeth.

CHAPTER SEVENTEEN

Elizabeth lived in a nice single-story house at the far end of Mt. Lookout. Her dad, Ernie, remodeled the outside of the home himself several years ago. The gray siding that used to be on the side of the house was looking shabby, and Elizabeth told me that her mom was complaining to her dad about it. Over a couple of months over one summer, her dad transformed the house from a dull, gray single storied dwelling to a very nice-looking log cabin. Nearly every hour that he was not working at his real job, he and his oldest son, Eric, were outside putting up this new log cabin façade. I don't quite know how he did the transformation, but I thought that the entire process was cool.

Ernie is a chemical engineer who works for the biggest chemical factory in the state, but he is also very good with his hands. Her mom, Edie, is a stay-at-home mom. She must be a very good one to have four kids and still be able to keep her sanity.

The home has a very nice basketball court her older brother Eric left behind. He now attended the state technical school in Montgomery. There is a large front yard where we often get together with people around the neighborhood during the summers to have a cookout and play some volleyball. She has an even larger backyard, which is also a nice gathering spot for many in the neighborhood. During the summer, Elizabeth's house is the place to hang out.

She has the older brother, Eric, and another much older brother named Eddie. She has a younger sister by the name of Erica, and her parents' names are Edie and Ernie. It's always been a running joke around the neighborhood that everyone calls the Evans family the E-Group or 'the Double-E's since everyone's name, first and last, started with the letter E.

By the time we ate pizza and finished our art homework, it was only seven o'clock. Elizabeth's family had retired to their family room to watch some TV while waiting for tonight's Monday night football game to start.

All the members of her family are football nuts. Even the women of the family loved football. It did not seem to matter which two teams were playing football. If there was a football game on television, they were going to watch it no matter who the opposing teams were.

While they were in the family room where the television was, Ashley, Elizabeth and I stayed in the dining room. They sat across the table from me. This felt like the same setup you see on cop shows on television. Where when they go to interrogate a suspect, they will take him into a cold, plain room with a steel table in the middle, three chairs, and a mirror running the length of one wall that everyone knows is a two-way mirror with the police chief sitting on the other side observing the interrogation.

I had that feeling as our evening shifted into a conversation that was more subdued. Like they were going to grill me.

Right now, the conversation was about what happened the evening I was in the hospital. I had told Ashley what I could remember about my brief stay. Elizabeth came to the hospital after her cheerleading practice ended, which wasn't long after I got there. She was now telling Ashley her version of the events that happened at the hospital, which I hate to admit, was accurate, and Ashley was thoroughly enjoying it.

Either this topic had not come up between them during my absence, or they were talking about this now to embarrass me. I could not imagine these two not talking about this, so I would say that this was for their entertainment.

"I and a couple of other people are sitting out in the waiting room, waiting to see Lucas," Elizabeth said. "Well, while we were all sitting there, we saw the door leading to the emergency room open, and a nurse was leading a very drugged up Lucas by the arm."

"I don't remember any of this, Ashley," I added. "The morphine that they gave me had me in such a haze that I didn't start remembering stuff until the next morning, much less what happened while I was at the hospital."

Ashley laughed.

"The nurse," Elizabeth continued, "led him right past where we were sitting. At this point," here she stopped and giggled before she could finish, "at this point, he's no longer wearing his football practice gear, but they have him in one of those backless hospital gowns, and his arm is already in a sling. I guess they were on their way to the x-ray room. As they walked past us, his gown must have caught a draft or something. Like Marilyn Monroe."

Ashley put her hand up to her mouth. "You didn't," she said to Elizabeth. I figured that she already knew what happened next, but I thought she was faking surprise for my benefit.

"Yes, I did." She looked me straight in the eyes, and gave me a long, drawn out, "Nice."

What ensued was at least two entire minutes of laughter at my expense.

"Okay, okay," I raised my hands in surrender when the laughter died down. "You got me. That wasn't my exactly my brightest hour."

"No, maybe not, but that was certainly one of the whitest butts that I have ever seen before," Elizabeth said and then added, "Not to mention the cutest."

"Well, thanks," I said with a little rouge appearing on my cheeks. "I don't know whether to be embarrassed, no pun intended, or flattered." This garnered more laughter from the two. I begged, "Can we change the subject, please?"

"Sure Lucas," Ashley said in such a way that maybe changing the subject might not be in my best interest after all. "When are you two going to hook up?"

My breath left me.

"You two who?" I asked, fearing what she was going to say.

Elizabeth was looking back and forth between Ashley and me, trying to figure out who the mystery girl was.

"Yeah, who?" she wanted to know.

"Why, the two of you, of course," pointing back and forth between Elizabeth and me.

To my total relief, Elizabeth didn't laugh. She appeared quite stunned, but I did not think she was going to burst out laughing.

"Listen," Ashley said, "Elizabeth, you've been my best friend ever since I can remember, and Lucas, you've been one of my best friends for a long time. I know you both very well. Elizabeth, you're the lead cheerleader…"

"Was," Elizabeth said.

"…was the head cheerleader," Ashley corrected herself. "And yet you've never had a boyfriend that has lasted for more than two weeks, and right now is one of those rare times where you don't seem to have a boyfriend. Lucas, have you ever had a girlfriend?"

I shook my head.

"I know that you have had opportunities, but you've never committed to any girl. I know why, but I bet Elizabeth doesn't."

I thought I was going to have a heart attack. My right arm was numb, and I thought that was one sign of a heart attack. It could just be that my arm was in a sling. I could see the years of Ashley keeping this secret for me ending. I hoped Elizabeth wouldn't fall over with laughter when Ashley revealed to her what I knew she was about to say.

I closed my eyes. I couldn't bear to watch.

"Elizabeth," Ashley said, "Lucas has had a crush on you since we were in all elementary school."

With my eyes closed tight, I heard a gasp escape from Elizabeth's lips. I still couldn't bear to look.

"Lucas. Look at me," Ashley said.

I opened one eye. Both girls were looking at me. Elizabeth looked rather shocked. I felt as though my face had gotten redder.

"The reason Elizabeth can't keep a boyfriend is because she keeps comparing every guy that she dates to you."

There it was. The heart attack. Did I really just hear that? I should not have been surprised judging from the warm reception she gave to me at school today. I guess that she really missed me while I was gone.

"W-why?" I managed to get out with my eyes fully open now, looking into Elizabeth's big, brown eyes. This was perhaps the stupidest question that I ever asked in my life. Deep down, I knew what the answer was.

"Because I've had a crush on you forever too," Elizabeth answered shyly, taking over for Ashley. "And every guy I've gotten close to, I don't stay close with for very long because none of them are as nice to me as you are."

All I could do was smile. I did not know what to say at this point. This was unfamiliar territory for me. I exhaled a breath I did not know I had been holding.

A pregnant pause came over the room.

Ashley broke it. "Look, I've known the two of you for years, and I've had to keep this a secret from the two of you for a long-time now, and as we were eating pizza, I thought, 'You know, I'm tired of having to do this. I think that I'm going to tell them both how they feel about each other.'"

"Thanks Ashley. I know that had to have been a burden on you." Elizabeth reached over and grasped her hand. I thought Ashley had a tear on her cheek. Wow.

"Yeah, thanks Ashley," I said. There was another awkward silence. Seeing her opportunity to leave, Ashley excused herself to the family room to watch the game with Elizabeth's family.

Elizabeth and I were alone. Now, with this revelation, it is as if we were alone for the first time.

***

Outside, the sky began to darken. Inside Elizabeth's dining room, the only illumination we had was the receding sunlight coming through the expansive bay window over Elizabeth's right shoulder.

"So, how long is forever?" I asked, breaking the silence.

"Oh. I don't know Lucas. I mean, when we were younger, in elementary school, I liked to sit near you in class because you had all the right answers, and you made me laugh. Your ears stuck out; your lips stuck out too. You had that bad cowlick in your hair, and you wore the goofiest glasses."

"Okay, okay. I get it," I said, holding my hands up in mock-surrender again. I was feeling like a murder suspect by having to raise my hands so much.

"Just let me finish," she smiled. "But you've grown into those ears and lips. The cowlick is gone and so are the glasses. And over those years where that happened, somewhere I stopped looking at you as the tall, goofy looking, smart kid from down the road, but as a tall, handsome, smart guy from down the road who I know for some odd reason, would do anything for me. And through all that you've done and helped me with, for some odd reason, I couldn't tell you how you made me feel."

"Well, I guess you can figure out why I've always hung around your older brother and have been at your every beck and call."

"Yeah," she said as she took a moment to assess all this new information. "I can see that now. Where do we go from here?"

"I don't know."

This was a lot of information for me to assimilate in five minutes. I always pictured us getting together, but I never imagined *how* it was going to happen. I never thought about what I would say if something like this were to happen.

"Why don't we talk about this tomorrow? It's getting late, and frankly, I just need some time to think."

"Yeah, me too, I've got a lot—we've both got a lot to think about. How about we talk about this at lunch tomorrow?" she asked me with a smile that I did not think that I had ever seen before. I could really like that smile.

"A 'lunch date'?" I asked.

"I think you could, yes," she smiled.

"Good. Well, let me collect Ashley, so we can get home. Ashley! Let's go!" I yelled into the other room.

I heard a faint, "Okay."

"How long have you been planning that?" I asked her as we settled into my car.

I looked over, and she had her head down, shaking it from side to side.

"You're not mad at me, are ya'?" she asked.

"No, I guess you were just tired of keeping secrets, huh?"

"Yeah, kind of," she shrugged. "I just thought that we're getting towards the end of our time in school, and if I didn't say anything, it would have been such a crime if you two had never gotten together. I just think that this way, at least you two know what each other thinks, and if it never happens, at least I won't have that on my conscience forever. What's going to happen to you two now?"

"I don't know." I put the car in gear and backed out of Elizabeth's driveway. "We're going to discuss it tomorrow and take it from there. I don't know about her, but I don't intend to get in any hurry about anything. We've only known about this for an hour, so there is no use in getting into any hurry about it."

The sun was gone. A thousand points of light hung in a cloudless sky overhead. We drove the short distance to Ashley's home with only the glow of my headlamps lighting the way.

I glanced over to see her silhouette shrug.

"Yeah, that's smart. No need to rush."

I detected some relief in her voice.

When we pulled into her driveway, I said, "I guess that I, we, am forever in your debt. I don't know what to say but "thank you." Thank you for keeping my secret for so long. Thank you for being such a good friend. Just . . . thank you."

In the darkness, I saw her smile. She leaned across the seat, and careful not to hurt my shoulder, gave me a big hug. "Thank you," she said, "for you being such a good friend as well."

"You're welcome."

"But I am sorry about one thing though," she said into my ear with her arms still around my neck.

"What's that?"

She pulled away from me, sniffled, and wiped a tear away from her eye. "For only being able to give you the second-best hug of the night."

The long hug Elizabeth gave to me before we left her house flashed through my mind.

With that, she collected her knapsack and got out of the car. I watched her walk to the front door, where she waved goodbye to me. As she stepped across the threshold into her home, I saw her wipe another tear away from her cheek.

I could only imagine how difficult this evening was for Ashley. I wondered at what point she decided that enough was enough.

I drove home with many thoughts and emotions racing through my mind. It must have been extremely hard on her to keep those secrets from us for these years. Maybe she was just relieved that it was over.

Elizabeth had liked me all along. This amazed me to no end. I know why I did not tell her about the way I felt about her. I couldn't imagine why with her outgoing personality she could not express the way she felt to me before now. I knew she had told other guys in the past the way she felt about them, but it didn't make sense why she couldn't tell me.

Maybe I shouldn't worry about it. My mind moved on to other more pressing subjects.

What was going to happen between us now? What were all of Ashley's tears about? Was she not happy to have that tremendous burden off her shoulders? Was she happy for us? Was there more to her story?

This last question occupied my thoughts on the way home. It was not until the middle of a sleepless night that I processed the rest of the evening's events.

CHAPTER EIGHTEEN

Jake had a normal evening at home with his folks. His mom made some delicious meatloaf. He did his homework and played video games for the rest of the evening.

When he finally crawled into bed, he could not seem to get to sleep. He had a lot on his mind. He had been doing okay by making a few friends since he had come here, but the friends that he had made were not really the kind of friends that he was aiming to make. They all seemed to be the types of guys, no girls yet, that didn't have very many friends. Loners. They seemed to look for someone to hang out with as well.

Jake was in the same position. He did not have very many buddies and was looking for someone to do something with. In the end, he wanted to get in with the popular crowd. He wanted to run with the fast crowd. He wanted to go to parties on the weekends or get dates with the popular chicks. Hanging out with these guys would not get him what he wanted.

He was having problems figuring out just how to make friends with some of the popular guys. There were three guys in his gym class he knew were on the basketball team, and they seemed to have a lot of friends. He tried to hang out with them during class and talk to them in the locker room. They never seemed to respond to him.

This one guy, Hunter, seemed to be the most popular of the trio. He was the one who seemed to pay Jake the least amount of attention. He seemed like some of the other guys from the schools he attended before that he would sometimes try to emulate. Hunter always seemed to have something to say that just sounded cool. There always seemed to be pretty girls around him. Hunter differed from Lucas. There was something about Lucas, though, that Jake wanted to be like as well.

Jake did not understand how Hunter did it, but maybe that was part of Jake's problem. Maybe Jake would have to make Hunter notice him. He did not know what that would be, but he could figure something out.

CHAPTER NINETEEN

The next morning, I went to school not having slept a wink. I tossed and turned the entire night. I dreamed about Elizabeth. Then I would turn over onto my shoulder and get jolted awake.

Somehow, I dodged traffic on the way to school without getting me or my friends killed. They were trying to figure out what was wrong with me. I figured that if I told everyone what happened to me last night that, they would laugh at me and not believe me, or they would believe me, and then tell everyone at school. Therefore, I only said that I could not sleep last night. This was still the truth.

When we got to school, I went to homeroom still groggy.

Elizabeth and Ashley were in their seats when I arrived in the room. Jake still had not made it in yet. His seat was still empty, so I took it. I would move whenever class started, or whenever Jake arrived, whichever came first.

"Good morning," I said as I sat down in Jake's seat in front of Elizabeth.

"Good morning, Lucas," they greeted me warmly.

"So, how'd you sleep last night?" Elizabeth asked me.

"Horribly. My shoulder was killing me."

"Aww, poor baby," Ashley said with a pout and then teased, "Are you sure it didn't have anything to do with what went on last night?"

"You might be on to something there," I said.

"Aww, how sweet," Ashley said, as if she were talking to a little baby.

I gave her another dirty look. The way we all thought of each other changed literally overnight. While we always got along before, now that the big secret was out, things seemed lighter. Easier.

Before Elizabeth could say anything else, a shadow crossed over my desk. I heard an impolite, "Ahem."

"Hey, Jake," I said, looking up.

"Hey. You're in my chair," he said brusquely.

"I wasn't aware that this was your property, but I was just leaving anyway."

This earned me a filthy look from Jake. I had the feeling that Jake does not like people violating his personal space though he seems to have no problems in violating other people's personal space.

I got up and raised an eyebrow at Ashley and Elizabeth. They had the same perplexed look.

"I'll talk to you at lunch," Elizabeth said.

I smiled and said, "Okay."

I walked over to my desk wondering what Jake's problem was. He didn't act like this yesterday. Except for the stare down he gave me and Elizabeth, Ashley, and I as were leaving school. This was the first time I had seen him in this kind of mood. I have only heard about it from a few others. I had rather limited my exposure to him since he moved here.

Except for when he broke my shoulder.

***

When your shoulder is in a sling, gym class is a waste of time as far as I was concerned. All I could do was sit by the bleachers, and either watch the activities going on, or study for one of my other classes. Today, I elected to study biology, as Coach Wheeler was probably going to give us a not-so-pop quiz. These quizzes seemed to happen every Tuesday.

The girl's gym teacher had them up in the mezzanines doing who knows what, leaving the guys with the entire gym floor to themselves. Out on the court, the guys were playing a game called Frisbee football. I wasn't sure why they put the word 'football' in the title. The game closer resembled soccer or hockey. In our gymnasium, there was a ten-foot section of padding on the wall about ten feet behind the two main basketball goals. The object of the game was to have someone successfully hit this padding with the Frisbee.

It's not as easy as it sounds.

Coach Nixon divided everyone into two teams, a blue or red team. He handed out colored vests to go over their gym clothes so everyone can differentiate who is on what team. The team in control of the Frisbee must pass the Frisbee from one teammate to the next without taking more than two steps in any direction. This kept people from simply charging at the padding. They flip it up the court from one end to the other without letting the other team intercept the Frisbee. When one team gets close enough to the goal, a person could attempt to score a point by hitting the padding with the Frisbee. Each team has a goalie always standing near the padding to keep this from happening. As I said, closer to soccer or hockey than football.

As Jake was the starting safety on the football team, and the only other players on the court from the football team are some of the slow linemen, Jake was the unequivocal leader of his team. There were a few other athletic guys that didn't play organized sports on his team, but he was still the unquestioned leader of the team from all outward appearances.

There were a few players from the basketball team out on the court, most of which were on the opposing team from Jake. Since they were getting into basketball season, they weren't playing very hard. Coach Nixon didn't seem to notice this and didn't push them to make more of an effort. Coach Wheeler would probably have Nixon's head if one of his players got hurt during some meaningless game in a gym class and missed actual game time.

Right now, charts and diagrams of cross sections of plants were what I was studying. We were studying photosynthesis again for like the fourth year in a row in science class.

I think it is a requirement for schools to waste taxpayer's money and the children's class time every year. They do this by teaching students the same things repeatedly. They just teach them a new wrinkle every year on whatever the topic was and say it's more advanced than last year's lesson. That way they can go home from school every day and tell mommy and daddy what the new thing was that they learned that day. Mommy and daddy will be impressed and continue to give the schools more and more support.

Schools should spend more time teaching us things we could apply to the real world after we graduate from school. They should teach us about how to refrain from violence, how not to break laws, how to become better citizens, friends, relatives, and eventually better parents. That should be the focus. Instead, they focused on teaching things such as photosynthesis, square roots, and where the medulla oblongata is in the human body. I realize some kids will eventually use some of those subjects, but they won't. As we proceed through high school, we, as students, should have a little more control of the classes we take as we look ahead to what we are going to do with our lives.

I'll get off my soapbox now.

Growing bored with the endless diagrams, I decided I would watch a little of what was happening on the court. I could not tell who was winning, but could tell that at least of a few of the guys were still trying hard. The ones still trying, from what I could tell, were the ones that were the sweatiest and had their hands on their knees trying to catch their breath when the action occurred away from them.

Currently, the team in control of the Frisbee was the team with red vests on. This team had some basketball players on it. Jake played defense and hovered near the goal, helping his goalie, hoping to intercept the Frisbee, which was pretty much his job playing football. Except here, he was not supposed to tackle anyone.

One of my best friends, Hunter, had the Frisbee. He was near the circle at the center of the basketball court. Hunter passed it to Tyler, who was near the sideline further up the court, closer to the goal.

The two decided they were going to run a basketball play and do a backdoor cut. Dillon was standing close to the guy covering Hunter. He took off in a sprint towards the goal. Dillon set a pick on Hunter's defender, enabling him to get free. Tyler knew what was happening and lofted the Frisbee in the general direction in which Hunter ran.

Hunter could leap higher than anyone I knew and has been dunking a basketball ever since the seventh grade. He's shorter than me, and I just recently got to where I could dunk a basketball.

Hunter saw the Frisbee coming his way, but everyone could tell that Tyler threw it a little high. No problem for Hunter. He leaped as high as he could to grab the Frisbee.

Then, from my perspective, everything started moving in slow motion.

I saw Jake come from halfway across the court at full speed and try to make a grab for the Frisbee. Instead, he collided with Hunter in midair, putting his forearm into Hunter's midsection, laying him out. He landed like a potato sack on the hardwood floor, with the back of his head making the first contact with a loud SMACK!

After this, everything sped up into a blur as Tyler and Dillon came to Hunter's defense. No one came to Jake's defense. I could see them pummeling Jake with their fists as he tried to defend himself. Hunter was on his feet now, but a little woozy. He saw what was happening, and I could see murder in his eyes, and he advanced towards the scrum.

Coach Nixon came in and pushed Hunter away so that he didn't do anything to get into any major trouble. Nixon grabbed

Tyler and threw him off Jake, where they had him pinned to the gym floor now. Then, he grabbed Dillon by the waist and tried to pull him off Jake, but not before Dillon hit him squarely, and very hard, on the right side of Jake's face.

The blow knocked him out cold on contact.

The gym was silent. The girls were standing against the railing up in the mezzanine, staring, and not quite believing, at what they just saw. No one else seemed to believe what they witnessed either, me included.

With the fracas over, Coach Nixon looked around, assessed the situation, and told Hunter, Dillon, and Tyler to go to the office. They stalked off in disbelief, as though they had done nothing wrong. Jake should be the only one getting into trouble.

Nixon had a few of the bigger guys in the class come over and carry the still unconscious Jake over to the bleachers near where I was. Nixon pulled some smelling salt from his pocket and held them under Jake's nose. He woke suddenly, but I could tell had no clue where he was, or what was happening.

Nixon then announced that class was over, and for everyone to go to the locker room and get showered and changed. We still had a good thirty minutes left of class, but I supposed that Coach Nixon had seen enough for one day.

When the bell rang, I left the gymnasium with the last image in my head of Nixon leaning over Jake whispering something to him, and Jake shaking his head, trying to clear away the cobwebs.

CHAPTER TWENTY

My Pre-Calculus class took place in a standard sized class-room at the end of the school, far away from the Commons Area. By the time I left that classroom, got halfway across the school to deposit my books into my locker, grabbed my lunch and arrived in the cafeteria, most everyone was already sitting down eating their lunches.

As I walked into the cafeteria from the entrance near the administrative offices, I looked to see if Elizabeth was at her customary table. She was, and I saw she had an empty spot beside her, which I assumed she was saving for me.

Elizabeth has a parenting class just before lunch. This class has the type of practical application in the real world I was thinking about before. It's not for the faint of heart, however, and not for me.

Anyway, her class was located just outside of the main doors of the cafeteria, and Elizabeth was usually one of the first people to receive her lunch. I could tell that by the time that I got there that she was already halfway through with whatever the mystery meat of the day was.

She looked up as I sat down. "Hey Lucas," she said with a smile. "How was your morning?"

"Very interesting, actually."

"Really?" She took a bite of her food. I saw her wince and briefly wondered if the mystery meat came from raccoons.

"Yeah, Jake picked a fight with some guys on the basketball team that are in my gym class. He got beat up badly. And if you'll look over there . . ." I said, pointing toward the principal's office. "You can see Jake, Dillon, Tyler, and Hunter sitting there waiting for who knows what."

Elizabeth's eyes followed the direction my finger was pointing to see the four through the windows in the office. Each of the four looked as though their favorite dog had just died. Except for Jake, he looked like hell *and* that his dog had just died. He was holding what looked like an ice pack firmly against his right eye. I could also see a nice red welt forming on his left cheek.

I thought this was odd. He seemed to have some sort of self-satisfied smirk across his face. I couldn't imagine what he could make him smile like that. He was probably going to be in some serious trouble. The other three guys didn't show any visible injuries or scars, but they all had their heads in their laps awaiting whatever punishment was going to be meted out by the principal, and later, and perhaps much worse, by their parents.

I looked over at Elizabeth. The scene in the office caught her attention. Her mouth formed a perfect, beautiful O. She snapped out of it when I started looking at her.

"What happened?" she asked.

I explained to her about the Frisbee football game that turned into a wrestling match before giving my predictions about what was going to become of the foursome sitting in the office.

"Well, none of them has ever been in any serious trouble before. I would say that Jake may get suspended for a few days for instigating the fight, and the other three will probably get detention if anything at all. After all, they were just defending Hunter, and if they're suspended, then they can't play in the season opening basketball game Thursday night's game against Webster County."

She looked thoughtful for a moment. "Makes sense to me."

"How was your morning?" I changed the subject to a much more pleasant subject: her.

"Certainly not as eventful as yours. Oh, but you should have been in my parenting class this morning!" she said excitedly, putting her hand on my arm. My good arm.

As I have already been over, parenting class was not my idea of an exciting class. If she got excited enough about it to put her hand on my arm, I could get excited too.

"Really?" I said with my eyebrows raised in mock excitement. "Why should I have been in your parenting class this morning?"

"Because we watched a video showing three different types of childbirth, and one of them was a C-section. It was wonderful!" She said this with full enthusiasm. She looked like a little girl describing her first trip to Disney World. I wasn't as thrilled with images of what she might have seen flooding my mind and making the mystery meat on her tray look less desirable. She must have seen the blank look on my face because she stopped smiling. "What? You don't think that childbirth is a beautiful, exciting event?"

I still could not respond. I did not know what to say to this. At my age, I still saw childbirth the way you see it happen in the old cartoons. You see a bunch of waiting men sitting in a waiting room at a hospital. A nurse comes running down the hall screaming, "Hot water! Hot water! Somebody, please get me some hot water!" Then a doctor comes out looking as if he had just made it to the hospital, coming up and congratulating the lucky dad. Then the dad hands out victory cigars. I think I saw it on an old episode of the Flintstones.

That did not sound like the way Elizabeth described it. I didn't know if I liked her way.

She gave me a serious look. "Honestly, that C-section was the grossest thing that I've ever seen." Then she grinned and gave my arm a squeeze. "Had ya going for a second, didn't I?"

"Y-yeah," I said. "You had me a little scared."

"It's okay. You're only a guy after all," she said, taking a drink of milk.

"So now I'm the squeamish one?" I asked. "Which one of us couldn't watch the second Hobbit movie because the first one made them so nauseous? "

"Touché,"

I emptied the contents of my brown lunch bag onto the table. Today's lunch consisted of a peanut butter and jelly sandwich, a Ho-Ho, a granola bar, and a box of Yoo-Hoo chocolate milk. The Lunch of Champions.

Elizabeth still had her hand on my arm, her lunch forgotten. I was trying to un-wrap my sandwich, and I could tell out of the corner of my eye that she was still staring at me. This made me nervous which made my task a little more difficult.

I wasn't doing a good job of unwrapping my sandwich. This was hard to do when a girl was resting her hand on one arm and the other one was in a sling. "What are you thinking about?" I asked, still struggling.

"You," she said playfully.

"What about me?"

"I think you look cute watching you trying to un-wrap that sandwich. Here, let me help." She grabbed the half open sandwich. She finished unwrapping it and handed it back. She licked a little jelly off her finger that got onto it from the sandwich.

That made my heart beat a little faster.

"Thank you," I said, taking a bite.

"But what am I thinking about?" she repeated my question. "Well, specifically, I was thinking about the two of us."

I would be lying if I told you I was not reading her mind. I do not know about her, but except for that fight this morning, I have thought of little else besides her.

"Ok, what about the two of us?" I asked. I'm so giddy that I think that if I didn't concentrate harder, was going to miss my mouth with my sandwich.

"Just where do we go from here, now that we know how each other feels?" she said with shyness. Or was it nervousness?

This subject had been foremost on my mind since last night. "I think that the first thing for us to do," I said, "is for us to go out on a date sometime. Not with friends or family. Just you and me. That way, we can get to know each other better outside of a group. But we've waited this long. I don't think that we should get in any hurry and screw this up."

"I agree. Why don't we go watch a movie Friday night? Maybe we can get something to eat before we go?"

I think that you just made my heart stop beating, I wanted to say. Instead, I said, "Sounds perfect."

"Great," she said. Sadly, she took her hand off my arm and resumed eating her now cold raccoon, I mean, mystery meat, I mean, chicken. Maybe. Probably.

I looked down at her right hand, which was the one grasping my arm, and saw it shaking ever so slightly. It was good to see that I was not the only one of us two that was nervous.

As we progressed through lunch, we discussed different things that we could do on our date. I thought it was such an accomplishment for me to get even an agreement for a date that for right now; I wasn't too worried about the details of said date. By the time lunch ended, we had made little progress as far as arrangements went.

CHAPTER TWENTY-ONE

Dinnertime around the Schofield house that evening was not a pleasant event for anyone involved.

His mom served up a good old-fashioned southern dinner she had learned from when they lived in the South. Juicy fried chicken, heaping piles of mashed potatoes and gravy, and, of course, buttery corn on the cob. This meal is what people often refer to as "comfort" food.

Indeed, there was little "comfort" to be received at this meal for Jake's parents or Jake.

When Jake's mom got the call from the secretary at school saying she needed to come pick him up because he had been suspended. She started to cry almost before she could put the phone back on the hook.

She was really liking Mt. Lookout and the Summersville area. She'd already made a few new friends from the immediate area around their new house and felt like there were some good people in the area. She liked her neighbors and some of the other people she had met while in Summersville. She hoped these people would be a positive influence on Jake.

It made her sad to think that this soon after they moved here, Jake would do something twice already to make her family look bad, and possibly give the appearance that her family should be avoided. The first full week they lived here, Jake had sent the high school's starting quarterback to the hospital, and now this. Getting into a fight with *three* other guys in gym class.

When Cherie arrived home with Jake in tow, she sent him up to his room for the afternoon, telling him he was not to watch any television. She yanked his X-Box out of the TV stand and left the room with cables dangling from the console. He did not argue, and he seemed to nap for much of the afternoon. She decided not to call her husband, Carl, at work. There was little that he could do. She may as well wait until he got home to tell him the news.

When Carl got home, and she broke the news to him, he did not seem to be surprised. He was upset, but not surprised. Cherie told him what the principal had told her, what had happened when she showed up to pick up Jake, but she had not gotten Jake's version of events yet. She told Carl that she wasn't strong enough to deal with the situation without his being here. She sent Jake to his room so she could avoid the situation until help arrived.

When Cherie had finished telling Carl what had happened, he gave her a hug and told her he wanted to hear what happened from Jake's standpoint before passing judgment. Cherie always felt that her husband had got into the wrong business and should have been an arbitrator instead. He was always good at wanting to hear both sides of the story before he made any judgment about anything or anyone. When he made his judgment, almost every time she could see the logic in his argument.

Carl waited until dinner to talk to Jake.

Jake had kept his head down with his hair covering his eyes while loading his plate with food. He tried at all costs to avoid eye contact or conversation. Cherie and Carl knew that this was going to be a hard task in getting Jake to talk about what happened.

"Jake," Carl asked, "could you pass me the mashed potatoes?"

Jake hesitated before reaching out to grab the bowl of potatoes. When he reached it over to his dad, Carl saw Jake's hand shaking from halfway across the table.

"I'm scared," Jake said.

Not showing any surprise at the question, Carl asked, "What are you afraid of, son?"

Jake, head still down, drew a breath, "I'm scared that I'm going to get in major trouble with you two, and I'm scared that now everyone is going to hate me at school."

Carl got a good look for the first time at the black eye that his son had received and the red welt that was on the side of his face.

"What makes you say that?"

"Because of what I did."

"What did you do?" Carl asked Jake as if this was the first that he has heard about anything. He looked across the table at his wife and made eye contact with her. She smiled knowingly. She knew Jake was taking a big step in talking about what happened openly instead of them having to draw it out of him.

"Did mom not tell you what happened?" Jake asked in disbelief.

"Yes, son, she did. But I wanted to hear your version of events before I decided about what to do about it."

Jake relayed his version of events that happened from his perspective. He told his dad that he was just going for the Frisbee and did not mean to tackle Hunter the way he did. He was not sure why everyone else started beating on him, but he pointed out that he did not fight back. He didn't mean to do it, and he apologized to Hunter while they were sitting in the principal's office. Jake said that Hunter and the other two boys ignored him.

"But, Jake, don't you think that there was a reason these other guys attacked you when you tackled this other kid?" Carl pointed out.

"Maybe they were still mad at me for screwing up Lucas' shoulder," Jake ventured.

Carl sat back in his chair, took a bite of the yellow corn, and looked thoughtful for a moment. "Son, I believe you."

Both Jake and Cherie looked surprised. In a soothing tome, Carl said, "Jake, with everything you've done, the one thing I can say is that you have always been honest with us about what happened. I have no reason to think that you are lying to us, and I can't see what these other guys would have done to provoke you into tackling this Hunter fellow. I would say that in some respects that you are correct in assuming that when these other boys jumped you, they were taking out their aggression over what you had done before.

"I remember when I was in school," he continued, "I played varsity football one year against our big rival. After one play when I was on the sidelines, one guy from the other team intentionally stomped on our All-State running back's ankle with his cleat after he had tackled him, and before our guy could get up. It snapped his ankle like a twig. Our entire defense was in a rage.

"The next time that they had the ball on offense, and I was out on the field playing defensive back like you do, Jake. They had a good receiver that shook himself free from another guy's coverage and caught a ball coming across the middle of the field. I saw an opportunity to shatter this guy. I saw he was going to jump up to catch the ball, and I had the chance to lay him out by going at him, helmet first. I was so angry that I almost did it. Instead, I put my arms around him while he was in the air and tackled him gently to the ground.

"I remember the look of fear in that boy's eyes when he turned around to look at me from his position on the ground. He figured I was going to get revenge for the gutless thing that his guy did to ours."

"What did you do?"

"I gave him a hand and helped him up and patted him on the backside as he went back to his huddle. Then, I congratulated him on making a good catch. You see, son, sometimes it's best to take the high ground when dealing with others. It sounds like these kids today didn't take the high ground. So, if that is their reasoning for attacking you today with little provocation, then these are the kinds of kids that you don't want to be around."

Jake looked thoughtful for a moment as he assimilated what his dad had told him. Then he asked, "So, does this mean I'm not in any trouble?"

"Oh, no, no, no," Carl said quickly, shaking his head. "I didn't say that. No, I'm going to say that you can't play video games, watch television, or go anywhere for a week."

Jake couldn't believe his luck. He had been dreading all afternoon the punishment that his dad was going to put on him. After what happened today, Jake figured his dad would decree that Jake would not see the light of day for a long, long time. "That's it?"

"That's it," his dad replied. "I figure that you've been through enough, and I don't think that any excessive punishment is necessary. I think you've learned that there are sometimes delayed repercussions for your actions." He looked at his wife from across the table, seeking her support in his decision.

She cleared her throat and said, "Yes, I agree with your dad, Jake. I think that you've been through enough. Now finish your dinner and go to your room."

"Thanks mom," Jake said, and put his fork into a piece of chicken.

When Jake had finished his dinner, his parents excused him to go to his room. Cherie made some coffee after Jake had left and set a steaming mug in front of her husband before resuming her position across the table from him.

"What are we going to do, babe?" she asked.

For the first time that evening, Carl looked tired. He shut his eyes and rubbed his temples before answering her, "Nothing for now, hun. I think that we have to trust our son's side of the story. To my knowledge, he's always been honest with us. When he has gotten into trouble before, he always tells the truth. I have no reason not to believe him. Now, if we find out that there was something more to his story than he is telling us, then we'll deal with it."

"I agree, babe. I just don't know how much more of this that I can handle," Cherie said, shaking her head.

"But you'll have to agree, he has gotten better lately."

"Oh, you're right about that. How long until something *really* bad happens again and we have to move along? Baby, I'm tired of moving. I just want to stay in one place for a long, long time." Tears started to drip into her coffee.

Carl stood up, came around the table, and wrapped his arms around his wife's shoulders.

"There, there hun. It's going to be okay," he said, kissing her on top of the head, and then took a deep breath. "If and when something happens again, we're going to stay here. I don't want to move again either, unless it's so bad that neither of us feels that we can face this town."

She broke the hug and smiled at him with a tear sitting on the corner of her eye. "Are you being serious?"

Carl put a hand to his chest. "Cross my heart."

"Thank you," Cherie said, reaching for his hand, and clutching his hand in hers.

"Anything for you, hun."

CHAPTER TWENTY-TWO

The principal suspended Jake for two days. Dillon, Hunter, and Tyler all were hit with a couple of days of lunch detention. This allowed them to play in the game Wednesday night against Webster County. They won that game easily, mainly because Webster County is a much less sparsely populated county than the one that we live in. Their school has about half as many people in it, so they have half as many students from which to field a team. That means their team is not as talented most years. Occasionally, they steal one from us.

I just want to inject here that basketball practice started a couple of weeks ago, but because of my shoulder, I wasn't healthy enough for the tryouts. Coach Nixon told me that because I could not try out, he wasn't going to let me play varsity when I returned to full health, but he would instead let me start on the Junior Varsity squad. However, they have already played one game and they have three more scheduled before I could even start practicing with the team. I may just sit this year out. It would hurt to do that. Basketball season is the thing that I look forward to most every year.

We ran late for school on Friday morning. By the time that we got to school, homeroom was already halfway over.

When Stone, Allen, and I came through the door, the room was silent. Everyone was intent on his or her studies, which meant one thing: Mrs. Gibson was on the warpath today.

Like many teachers, Mrs. Gibson brings her home life to school with her. If bad things are happening between her and her husband, as they frequently do, every person in her classes knows about it. When you live in a small town like ours, if somebody was doing something they should not be doing, such as drinking too much alcohol, having an affair, getting into a fight, etc., word spread rapidly.

It was no surprise that when word got out about her husband's alleged infidelity, the whole town knew about five minutes after Mrs. Gibson knew. You could tell a remarkable difference in her teaching style. She went from being one of 'your best friend' types of teachers to 'your worst enemy' type of teacher immediately.

At the start of a class when she was on the warpath, you could always count on receiving some sort of topic for an essay that was just totally out of this world in which you could never hope to make any sense in your essay; much less get it completed by the end of class. During these times, there would be absolutely no talking and absolutely no bathroom breaks.

The first time that this happened to me, I was in her American History class. She came into the room, looked at the class that had suddenly gone deathly silent at her entrance. We could sense her ill mood. Before she went back to her desk, she wrote on the blackboard in huge, angry letters:

The Industrial Revolution was neither Industrial nor a Revolution.

Tell me why in 1000 words by the end of the period.
USE YOUR TEXTBOOKS FOR RESEARCH!
NO BATHROOM BREAKS OR TALKING!

She then stomped to her desk at the rear of the room, collapsed into her chair, and put her head down on the desk. All the students were so scared that they dared not to speak. I have seen her this way once or twice since then, but I am just glad that I am not in any of her classes this semester.

These past two days have been as perfect for me as you could imagine. You just have to put yourself in my shoes. They were as perfect as you could imagine for a teenager who has his arm in a sling, had two big tests in Pre-Calculus and Biology to study for, and had a visit from his great aunt.

I had never met him before. She flew in from Texas for a surprise visit. If I never hear another story about a 2 a.m. calf birthing, it will not be too soon. Now I know why my mother rarely ever spoke of her.

No, the past two days have been so ideal because I have spent some time talking to and getting to know Elizabeth more. I have learned things about her over the past two days that, just growing up from her down the street, I never knew or guessed.

As Allen, Stone, and I entered the room, I saw Ashley had her head buried in a psychology textbook. Elizabeth was just glancing through what looked like an algebra book. She looked up at me as I passed and gave me a sweet little smile. I noticed Jake had returned to school after his two-day absence. He had a black eye, which made him funny to look at.

Before I could sit down, Mrs. Gibson called from her desk without looking up, "Boys, you're late." As if this was news to us. "This is the second time this semester. If it happens again, I'll have to send you to the office for lunch detention," she said with a shadow of rage in her tone.

"Yes, ma'am," we said in unison and sat down.

I had just enough time to open my biology book before I heard, "Thanks a lot," whispered into my ear by Allen.

"Mr. Wyrick," Mrs. Gibson said as if she had the hearing of canines, "would you like to go to the office now?"

I thought I heard Stone snort a laugh. Thankfully, Mrs. Gibson did not hear him. I stiffened up, and I could sense Allen do the same behind me. Allen likes to argue with people, especially grown-ups. I do not think that Allen could win this potential fight. I hoped he wouldn't reply with 'What for?'

"What for?" he asked.

I lowered my head. I foresaw that this was going to be a long morning for Allen.

"Just be quiet," I wanted to say to him, but didn't.

"Well, Mr. Wyrick, you're disrupting my class time, your peers' study time, and your study time."

"I just said one thing to him," Allen argued and then made the one mistake you never make with a teacher, especially a teacher who is just not in a good mood. He ended with this retort, "Gosh!"

"I guess you want to go on to the office," Mrs. Gibson said, raising her voice. "Go down to the office and tell Principal Dunlap that I'll be down there after the bell rings!"

Without a word, Allen slammed his book shut and stormed out of the room. I will place 50/50 odds on Allen even reaching the office. I will also place 50/50 odds on Mrs. Gibson even going down to the office herself. This has happened on occasion with both. I have seen Allen get sent to the office. He would not bother and end up in the gym playing basketball. This often landed him in more trouble than he would have been in to begin with.

As I mentioned, this isn't the first time I've seen Mrs. Gibson in this sort of mood. She will send a student to the principal's office, tell them she will be there at the end of the period, and not show up, letting the student sit in the office for a few hours. I do not know if she forgets she sent the student to the office, or just wants the student out of her class for the rest of the period.

As Allen reached the doorway, the bell sounded. He looked back at Mrs. Gibson, wondering what to do. Nobody had made a move to leave the room yet watching the drama unfold. Everyone had turned around in his or her desks to see what is going to happen next.

"Go to your next class, Mr. Wyrick," she said, waving a hand dismissively.

"Thank you!" he said, scurrying away.

With the drama over, everyone gathered their things and filed out of the room.

I closed the unread biology book and walked over to Elizabeth's desk, where she was getting out of her chair. "Hey," I said.

"Hey Lucas. Where were you at this morning?"

"Oh, you know. I overslept." I yawned to show the evidence.

"Oh really. I thought you said that your mom was your alarm clock. How could you oversleep?"

"Okay, okay. You got me. Blake spent too long in the bathroom this morning," I said in my defense. She raised an eyebrow. "Okay, I spent too long in the bathroom."

"That's what I figured. Are we still on for tonight?"

"You bet. Do you want me to walk you to class?" I extended my left arm.

"I would be honored," she said in her most regal voice, taking my arm. She already had her English books with her for her first period class and I have gym class first period. The English is on the other side of the school away from the gym, so it's a little out of my way for me to walk her to her class, and then get to the gym in time before the bell rings. I could handle it.

As we walked down the hallway, we caught a few stares from our other classmates who had never seen us together in this way before. If we were not a gossip item before today, I was sure that we would be by lunchtime. As I mentioned before, it's a small town.

I told her we were going to the nicest restaurant in town, Applebee's. There are not a lot of restaurants to choose from and it was that Applebee's is the only restaurant of choice in town for a romantic date. If you have ever been to Applebee's, then you know that this is a sad commentary on our little town. Then after that, we were going to see any movie she chose. She seemed delighted. When we reached the door to her classroom, she unlatched herself from my arm and gave me a quick hug. Then she said in an accent suited for a Jane Austen film, "Thank you, kind sir. I will see you at lunch."

"You're welcome, Miss Evans. Have a splendid morning!" I said as I backed away down the hallway, tipping my imaginary top hat.

I saw Hunter round the corner of the hallway. He saw me as I tipped my imaginary cap. He did not seem to display any ill effects from his fight in the gym the other day with Jake.

In fact, he seemed on top of his game. He looked at me, put a hand on my shoulder and said, "Lucas, I'm going to have to take your Man Card after seeing that. I don't think we can even be friends anymore."

Since I had known Hunter for a couple of years now, I let the comment pass.

"Whatever. Who are going out with tonight?" I asked.

It took him a moment, but I saw the lights come on in his eyes. The smile faded. Fast. "No. You're not going out with her."

"Yup," I said with a bit of bravado.

"Oh, you go boy!" he said, giving me a low five, slapping my hand. We walked the rest of the way to the gym together. The smile returned to his face.

I could tell from how Hunter was now dancing around that he may be more excited than I was about my date tonight. He tried to hook me up with several girls over the past few years, but he could never figure out why I would date none of them. It would be impossible for him to be any more excited than I am right now. I was so giddy with pent up excitement over tonight that I just wanted this school day to be over as quickly as possible.

***

My shoulder was healing up rather nicely. During gym class, I took part in the warm-up exercises, except for the pushups, and shot some baskets at one end of the basketball court while the rest of the class was learning the art of Greco-Roman wrestling on the mats up in the mezzanine. I was told later that Jake was forbidden to wrestle with any of the guys that he got in that fight with the other day. I was sure that disappointed Jake and the other participants immensely. Male aggression being what it is and all.

When I need time to think, or if I am upset at something, shooting baskets has always been the tool I used to get my head clear or think about stuff. Say that I have some problem at home, and one of my parents yells at me for no apparent reason. Instead of arguing back or letting it get to me, I just go outside into my front driveway and shoot baskets for a while. It's therapeutic.

As I shot the basketball, I thought of only one thing: my date with Elizabeth. I have never been out on an actual date before. I do not know what to do. I just hoped that I did not make a fool out of myself. Somehow, with Elizabeth, I did not feel that it would be a problem. Besides Ashley, Elizabeth was the only girl I felt I could be myself around and not come off seeming to be a weirdo. When I am around girls, I sometimes feel weird talking to them, and I never really seem to say the right things. I felt safe in knowing that Elizabeth and I have been good friends since I can remember, and that if she does not think that I am a weirdo by now, she's not going ever going to. At least I hoped.

My previous relationship with her wasn't what was worrying me right now. I was more worried about minor details, things that I am ignorant about with dating. What should I wear tonight? Do I order for her? Was it appropriate to hold her hand during the movie on a first date?

The only person who I know I can ask these kinds of questions to would be Ashley, but I didn't know how she would react coming to her for advice on this topic, considering how she reacted before. I couldn't ask any of my guy friends about this because they will all try to tell me the best way to get her to make out with me. Not that I do not want to do that, not at all. That'd be great. I just didn't want to rush anything. I've waited this long to pursue a relationship with her, that I didn't want to do anything that might damage our relationship or make her think I was like all the other guys.

I was in such deep thought that I failed to notice Jake standing beside the court watching me shoot. I shot a three-pointer that ricocheted off the side of the rim and bounced towards the sideline on the opposite side of the court to where Jake was standing.

He caught the ball and tossed it back to me. "Brick," he said flatly.

"Thanks," I said as I snagged the pass. I turned and shot. It bounced a few times on the rim before falling through. By the time I turned around, I saw his back going through the double doors leading to the locker room.

As I watched the doors close behind him, I foresaw a storm brewing.

CHAPTER TWENTY-THREE

During art class that afternoon, Elizabeth and I finalized our arrangements for that evening. We agreed that I would pick her up at around six thirty. From there, we would go have dinner and then catch whatever movie she wanted to see.

After school let out, she gave me a hug before she got in the car with her mom. When I reached my car, I saw my brother, Brian, Allen, and Stone all standing in front of the car waiting for me. They looked like they were freezing, and they probably were. None of them had coats. The temperature didn't reach forty degrees today. I had yet to tell them about my date with Elizabeth. They knew something was up but didn't know what.

On the way home, they discussed their plans for the evening.

"There's a party over at Tommy Abrams' house," Stone said. "I might check that out. Anybody interested?"

"Sure, I'll go," Brian said. He turned to Allen, "You?"

"Na, I just got the new Madden game," Allen replied. "I think that I'll just stay at home and play that all evening. Blake, you can come over and play if you want to."

Stone looked at my brother. "What about you, Blake, party or video games?"

Blake liked the occasional beer, but I know he would not pass up an evening to play video games for almost any reason. Like clockwork, Blake replied, "I think I'm more up for some Madden myself."

Stone sitting behind me clapped me on my good shoulder. "What about you, big guy? Want to go have some fun tonight? I know you don't ever go to these things but come on. Sometimes you have to cut loose! What do you say?"

"Na," I replied, focused on the road.

Allen liked that answer. He thought he was getting another potential football player. "Alright! Me and the Caine brothers for an all-night Madden Marathon!"

"Na," I said to that suggestion as well.

Everybody looked at me while I was trying to concentrate on the traffic heading away from the school. "What are you going to do? Read a book?" Stone asked. Then under his breath he said, "Nerd."

"Hey, I heard that," I said. "No, for your information, I already have plans for this evening."

"Really? That's a first. Do your 'plans' include staying home and reading a book or something?" Brian said.

In the past couple of years, I have begun reading books. I had no interest in books when I was younger. On Sundays during the summer months, a lot of my friends and relatives from around Mt. Lookout will go to the baseball field at the elementary school and play softball if the weather permitted.

One particular week, during a summer a couple of years ago, I somehow contracted a freak summer flu. I had a fever of over one hundred degrees. I could not stop coughing. My head felt like it was being squeezed between two vise grips. I felt horrible. I sat out that Sunday's softball game.

That afternoon, while my friends were at the elementary school playing softball, I sat down on the couch to see what was on TV. The only appealing thing on TV was that the Sci-Fi Channel was showing the original Star Wars trilogy back-to-back-to-back. I had always heard that they were good movies but had never watched them. I sat back on my couch, with a blanket over my legs, with my mom bringing me cup after cup of hot tea and watched the whole trilogy. It was the most amazing thing I had ever seen.

When I go to the supermarket with my mom, I read magazines from the magazine rack during the time she shopped. Beside the magazine rack, they always had a display of best-selling novels. I always looked at them, but nothing ever caught my eye. After watching the movies, I remembered seeing a new Star Wars novel on that bestseller display. The following week, when we went to the grocery store, I picked it up.

I loved it. I loved it so much that I have now read like twenty Star Wars books based on the movies. My mom would let me read some of the regular fiction books that she had, and I loved them too. So now, I am about the only guy that I know that reads one or two books a week. When I was home from school those two weeks with my broken collarbone, I read something like ten books. So now, everybody calls me a "bookworm." I don't mind. I take it as a compliment.

In reply to Brian's derogatory statement, I said, "No. That sounds nice. But I have a date with Elizabeth this evening."

A few of the guys cheered, the others laughed just as I figured they would do. They had all seen me spending some extra time with Elizabeth this week, but I do not think that they thought she would go out with me.

Stone, one of the cheerers, said to me, "Well congrats, man. We've been seeing you spend more time with her this week than you did with us. It's good to see you get out of the house for once, though, especially to go out on a date."

"Yeah," the rest of the guys agreed.

Brian seemed to ponder something for a second. "Hey Lucas, I was wondering about something. Is this your first date, ever?"

"Yeah," I answered.

"Alright, it's about time," he said and punched me on the bad shoulder. I winced in pain. "Oops, sorry man, maybe you can have Elizabeth rub on it this evening."

Everybody in the car had a good laugh at my expense.

I smiled at that thought of that for the rest of the way home.

***

The clock ticked.

One hour before I was to pick up Elizabeth, I was sitting in my boxers, on my bed, staring at three different outfits I had picked out for this evening. I had been staring at these same three outfits for about half an hour, still with no clue which one is the perfect one for this evening. I didn't want to ask my brother about it.

When it comes to women, he is about as clueless as they come. I did not want to ask my mom about it either. That would be embarrassing. I would ask my dad, but he was still at work, and wouldn't be home until after I left. He was a snazzy dresser, and his advice would really come in handy right about now.

Outside, the temperature was just barely above freezing, so I picked three warm outfits. The first two involved khaki pants of different shades and two different button-up shirts. One outfit has a tie that I could put with it. The other outfit is just a pair of blue jeans and a nice off-white colored sweater I picked up from J-Crew the last time that I went into the city.

I didn't know whether to go for a formal or casual look for this date. I had an idea who might know. I reached over, picked up the phone from my nightstand, and called Ashley's cell phone. It rang twice before she answered.

"Hello?"

"Hey Ash," I said. "What's up?"

"Not much, just doing some homework. What's up with you?"

"Aw, not too much," I said, playing it down. "I'm just trying to get ready for this date."

"Oh, I take it by 'trying' you mean you don't know what to wear," she said. I think she knew what I was calling her for.

"Ashley, I think you know me better than I know myself sometimes. But you're right. I've been staring at the same three outfits now, going on forty minutes. I'm completely clueless. Help?" I begged.

Ashley has been dating guys for years, so if there's someone that I know that would qualify to give advice for first date dress attire, it would be her.

"Describe to me what you have picked out," she said, all business now. She was in her territory. I briefly described the three outfits that were before me.

"Are you going to be wearing the sling?" she asked. I told her I wouldn't be. She thought about it for about two seconds. "Go with the jeans and sweater."

"The jeans and sweater? Are you sure?" I asked, taken aback by how fast she decided.

"Of course, I'm sure. Listen, I know Elizabeth, and I know that she's not going to be impressed by the more formal clothes. I also know you. I've never seen you in a button-up shirt and a tie outside of church. Besides, I know what sweater it is that you're talking about. You look pretty good in it."

My cheeks warmed. I was glad that we weren't in the same room together. "Thanks."

"Besides, I know what Elizabeth is wearing. She called me up about ten minutes ago, asking the same question. That's kind of why I figured you were calling about what to wear."

"You're so smart, Ashley," I told her as I walked over and picked up the advised outfit.

"Aww, it's nothing. Look, I think that both of you are nervous. So I'm going to tell you what I told her."

"What's that?"

"Just remember that you two have known each other for years, and that you two have been out in social situations like this all the time. It's just that this time, there's not going to be anybody else there. Just you two. Think of this as one of those times."

I thought about it for a few seconds. She was right. I shouldn't be worried about anything.

"Ashley, you're the best. You don't know how much I appreciate this. I'll pay you back, I swear!"

"You mean that?"

"Yeah, of course I do. You know that I'm a man of my word. You just name it."

"Oh, don't worry about it right now," she answered. "You just go on your date, and don't think about anyone else except Elizabeth."

"Thanks," I said. "Do you have any last-minute advice?"

"Just one thing," she said. "I think that she's going to be wearing an overcoat. When you get to your table at the restaurant, pull out her seat for her, and then take the coat off her before she sits down."

"What do I do with the coat?"

"I don't know. Just lay it over the seat next to you," she sighed. "Look, don't get caught up in the details. Focus on her. Think about how special it will make her feel. Everyone in the restaurant will look at you two for about ten seconds when you go to sit down. You will make her the center of attention. Believe me, she'll like it. Just have fun."

I could imagine the scene in my head. It sounded perfect.

"Ashley, you are a genius! Thanks so much!" I said and hung up the phone.

I put on the recommended outfit. I went into the bathroom and brushed my teeth. I didn't have any cologne myself, but I knew my dad kept some in the medicine cabinet. I looked in there to see what he had. All I could see was a bottle of Chap's aftershave. I pulled the cap off the top and took a whiff. It didn't smell too bad, so I splashed some on my neck and wrists. I ran a brush through my hair and checked the mirror to make sure that everything was straight.

Not too shabby, I thought. I would have to thank Ashley again.

I rehearsed what I would say to Elizabeth when I got to her door a few times while looking into the mirror. Satisfied that I wouldn't make a fool out of myself, I went downstairs, grabbed my keys, and put on my coat. Of course, getting something to sound perfect in your head is one thing. Getting your mouth to produce those words, in that order, with the intended inflection, doesn't happen very often.

My mom met me at the door. She reached up and grabbed me by the shoulders. She smiled. "Lucas, I'm glad that you've finally gotten the nerve up to go out with that cute Elizabeth."

"What do you mean 'finally'?"

"Your father and I have known that you've been smitten with Elizabeth since you were both little kids."

"But how did you know?" I asked her. I didn't know how she would know. My crush on her was not something that I broadcast to everyone, especially not to my parents.

"We could just tell by looking at you every time that we see you around her. You're always so googly-eyed, and don't know what to say. We've seen that look many times before. And when you speak of her, you speak of her with a bit of reverence. You speak of her like she's the president's daughter. And when you speak to her on the phone, you seem more tongue-tied that usual. We just know Lucas," she explained.

Feeling a little awkward, I glanced at my watch. My mom caught on to what I was doing and said, "Okay Lucas, I get it. Time for you to go. You go on your date and have fun. But be back before eleven."

I mirrored her smile. "Thanks, I will." I gave her a hug and then left for my date.

***

I arrived at Elizabeth's house five minutes before I was supposed to pick her up. Outside of school, I like to be punctual. I got out of my car and walked up the sidewalk that led to her front door. It was getting cold out. I had to rub my hands together just to get a little warmth to them. I thought that I should have worn a heavier coat.

I wiped my shoes on her welcome mat, and then lightly rapped on the door. Her father answered the door almost immediately.

"Hey Lucas," he said. He had a deep voice and a cultured accent. Not British. Not Ivy League. But you could tell he was a well-educated man. I'd have to be even more on my guard than usual. "Come on in. Elizabeth will be ready in a few minutes. Besides, it's too cold for you to be standing out here. Come on in," he repeated, "I have a fire going."

"Thanks." I said, as I walked in and followed Mr. Evans across the room to the fireplace, where he had the small fire blazing.

"Have a seat Lucas," he gestured at a chair that he seemed to have picked out for me. He took a seat across from me beside the fire, grabbed a poker, and stoked the fire. I hoped he wasn't trying to send me a message.

He set the poker aside and leaned back in his recliner. He stared at me for a moment, while folding his hands across his stomach. I looked down and noticed his partially mutilated right hand. He was entirely missing his ring finger, and his middle finger was slightly, but noticeably crooked.

It happened when I was in middle school. I was riding the bus to school one morning—I think it was on a Monday—and one of the older high school kids got on the bus. I knew he was a classmate of Elizabeth's older brother. He came back and started telling me about what happened to Mr. Evans over the weekend.

He said that he was helping Mr. Evans and his sons work on a storage shed they were building to put lawnmowers, yard tools, etc. in. Mr. Evans was using a circular saw to cut some lumber and accidentally cut off his middle and index fingers on his right hand. The doctors reattached the middle finger, but the ring finger was a lost cause. I remembered how horrified I was and how sorry I felt for him.

We engaged in some small talk while we waited for Elizabeth to get ready.

"Lucas," he said during the conversation, "as you go through your life, you will learn some very important things about women, hopefully. But I'm going to tell you something that you may not know about women yet."

I leaned forward in my chair and looked directly at Mr. Evans. "Yes, sir, what is it?"

He waves his hand dismissively. "Now Lucas, you have never called me 'sir' in your life. You don't need to start with the formalities now just because you're taking my oldest daughter out on a date tonight. Don't be nervous. It's not me you have to impress this evening. It's that little lady somewhere down that hallway that you need to put the charm on for."

I exhaled slowly. One less thing to worry me.

He continued, "Lucas, I have always liked you. I've always thought that you were a very upright young man. I've never heard of you going to these parties that these kids throw nowadays. I've never heard of you getting in trouble at school, or anything like that. I've always kind of hoped that you would take an interest in Elizabeth. That's just between me and you," he added conspiratorially. "I was happy, and surprised, when Elizabeth asked me for permission to go on this date with you."

"That's what my mom said," I told him, making him laugh. "What is this secret about women you were going to tell me about?"

He leaned forward in his chair and looked me dead in the eye. "The first thing that you have to know about women in a relationship is that no matter when you get ready to go somewhere, it doesn't matter where you are going, you're always going to be waiting on the woman to get ready. It's one of those givens in life: death, taxes, and waiting on women. Just don't ever let on that it bothers you."

"Don't listen to him, Lucas. He's just an ignorant man," I heard Elizabeth's voice come from over my shoulder.

I turned and stood up in one motion to greet her. When I saw her, she took my breath away.

She had her blond hair pulled up and tied back with a few strands of hair that fell over her face. This is my absolute favorite way for a girl to wear her hair. To me, there's not a sexier look. She wore a light touch of makeup, with a little pink lip-gloss. She also had some small diamond earrings dangling delicately from her earlobes. She wore a blue and white striped cardigan sweater with horizontal stripes over a nice pair of navy dress pants. Her look was simple, elegant, and considering the occasion, easily one of the most beautiful sights that I have ever laid eyes on. If this was Ashley's suggestion that she dressed like this, I was going to have to give her a huge thank you.

"Well, hey, Elizabeth," I said with a huge, unconcealed smile on my face. There was no way I could hide it.

"Well, hey to you too," she said, looking me up and down, giving me a look of approval. "Have you been waiting long?"

I looked over her shoulder and saw Mr. Evans shake his head. "Just sat down," I said to her. "Are you ready to go?"

"Yeah, just let me grab my coat."

I let her go out the door first. After her exit, I looked back at Mr. Evans. "Thanks for the advice."

"You're welcome, Lucas. You two try to be careful, have fun, and be back by eleven o'clock." He looked thoughtful for a moment, then confided to me, "But if you're a few minutes late, I won't tell anyone."

I thanked him and turned to hurry down the steps after Elizabeth.

I caught up with her, and she hooked her arm in mine while we were walking the short distance to my car. "What was that about?"

"Just some guy talk," I answered.

She seemed satisfied by the answer and asked no follow-up questions. We reached my car, and I opened her door for her. She gave me a smile as she slid into the front seat. I shut the door and ran around to the driver's side.

I started the engine and cranked up the heat. "Thanks," she said. "It's freezing in here."

"My car warms up pretty fast, so it shouldn't take long to get you warm." I put the car in gear and backed out of the driveway. "Here we go," I said to myself. "No pressure."

"Huh?"

"Oh, nothing, just talking to myself," I explained vaguely.

"Well, just so long as the voices don't start answering you back, you'll be okay," she joked.

"When that happens, I'll really be in trouble." I flicked on the headlights. "But for now, it's just me."

"You're silly," she stated playfully. "C'mon, I'm hungry. Let's eat."

"I agree. I am so starved right now," I said, rubbing my stomach.

CHAPTER TWENTY-FOUR

When we arrived at the restaurant, the parking lot was mostly full, but I found a parking space close to the door. When we went in, there was no waiting. The hostess led us through the restaurant with menus in her hand.

"Will this be okay?" she asked, waving at a table out in the open area of the restaurant. I looked over at the wall, hoping to spot a vacant booth. There were none.

"This will be fine," I said to her. She laid two menus and glossy inserts advertising the current specials on the table and departed.

I took out Elizabeth's chair, and before she sat down, I helped her out of her jacket, as Ashley suggested. It got the response I had hoped. She beamed and thanked me. Elizabeth was the focus of this entire section of the restaurant. She ate it up. I could tell she felt special.

After I draped our coats across a chair, I sat down. She looked at me. "Thank you, Lucas. I felt like everyone was staring at me. That gave me goose bumps." She rubbed her hand up and down her forearm, which gave *me* goose bumps. "I kind of liked it," she smiled.

We settled in and started looking over our menus. Now we were at a point where I did not know what to say. Before the date, I rehearsed everything I would say when I first saw her, opened her door and different scenarios on how the evening might end. I never stopped to consider that we'd have to make small talk. Thankfully, Elizabeth has had practice and led the way.

"Do you want to start with an appetizer or something?" she asked without looking up from her menu.

I thought about the forty dollars I had in my wallet. I had to factor in the cost of dinner here, the price of two movie tickets, and something my dad referred to as "inflation." Whatever that meant. Then what if she wanted a drink and popcorn at the theater? Those would cost almost as much as this dinner. I made the decision that we could forego the appetizer,

I felt hunger pains when we left her house. I hadn't eaten since I had a sandwich at lunch. Since then, nerves set in. Those hunger pains became waves of nausea. I felt that a large dinner might have some . . . awful consequences.

"No, I'm not all that hungry. Let's get what we want for our meal." I said, putting together two consecutive sentences without stuttering or stopping. It was a small personal victory. I hoped my suggestion was okay with her.

"Yeah, I'm not that hungry either," she said, eyes still on her menu.

"But you can order whatever you want to," I said.

"Thanks, but I don't want much myself. I was thinking about just ordering a big salad," she said, looking up from her menu. I stared at her for a moment without realizing it, and I glanced at my menu so the moment didn't get too awkward. My tongue felt heavy in my mouth.

"Go right ahead," I said, just now really studying my menu for the first time. "I might just get some kind of grilled chicken."

"That sounds good," she said, thinking hard. "Tell you what. I'm not all that hungry myself. If you like, order whatever you want, and maybe we can split it?"

That would take some pressure off my funds but put a lot of pressure on me to pick something that she would like.

Our server walked up to our table and introduced herself as Irene. She apologized for taking an extra minute to get to our table. "Can I take your drink order?" Elizabeth ordered sweet tea. I did the same. "Are you two ready to order your food, or do you need a few more minutes?"

I glanced at Elizabeth. She nodded. "Yeah, I think we're ready. We're going to split a plate of the parmesan chicken."

"Do you want to add a salad to that?"

I looked at Elizabeth, and she nodded her head in a negative. "No. That will be all Irene. Thanks."

"You're welcome," she said as she collected our menus before departing.

"Good choice," Elizabeth said. "I was hoping for some Italian food this evening."

"That's good," I said, relieved. "I was hoping I wouldn't order something you didn't like."

"Well, you can't go wrong with chicken smothered in mozzarella cheese and marinara sauce, sitting on a bed of spaghetti," she laughed.

I laughed too, nervously. I knew she had a healthy diet, but perhaps she wanted to live a little tonight.

We sat silently for a few moments. I looked around at the rest of the diners with my hands grasped on the table in front of me. The crowd seemed to be mostly older to middle-aged people. I didn't see anyone that might be our age. This was good. It meant less gossip at school.

The patrons were well dressed in a casual sort of way. This was good. At least now, I didn't feel over or underdressed.

I felt Elizabeth grasp both of my hands in hers. I looked at her in surprise. "Hey, I'm over here. Remember me, you're date?"

I smiled. Time to turn on the charm. "Of course I do. I was just looking around, making sure that my hunch was correct."

"And what 'hunch' is that?"

"Oh, I was just making sure that you were the prettiest girl here." She looked down in embarrassment, but she was smiling. I struck a chord. "My hunch was correct."

"Aww, Lucas, you're too much."

I turned the charm up a notch. "In fact, I'd go so far to say that you're the absolute, most beautiful girl that I've ever seen from how you look tonight."

Her cheeks flushed in a way I couldn't remember seeing before with her.

"Lucas, I don't know what to say. No one has ever told me anything like that." She looked close to tears.

"I wouldn't say it if it weren't true." She squeezed my hands a little tighter. I will never confess how long I practiced that line in my head. I am nowhere near smooth enough to come up with that line on the spot. I looked down at her two small hands covering and squeezing my two much larger hands. "I like the red nail polish, by the way."

She laughed and sniffled at the same time. That seemed to break the ice. I wanted to giggle but held back. "Thanks Lucas. You've always been so sweet."

"You're welcome," I said, now the one that was embarrassed.

The waitress brought our drinks and told us the rest of our order would be out soon. I put a straw in my drink and saw my hand shaking.

Apparently, she noticed as well, and grasped my hand after I put it back on the table. "Look, Lucas, I know that you're nervous. But don't worry about anything, it's just me. I'm not going to be supercritical of everything that you do or say this evening. We're just two friends who have known each other for a long time, maybe looking to take our relationship somewhere else."

This made my pulse slow down. A little.

"Lucas, do you remember when we were in kindergarten together?" she asked. I nodded. "Do you remember the nap times that we had after recess, when the teacher would get out the little mats for all the kids to lie on? And she would go out and have her afternoon smoke break while we were supposed to be napping."

"Yeah, those were the days. It seemed all we did was play in that class."

"Yeah," she continued, "but that's not what I'm talking about. Do you remember the kids you were near during those naptimes? Did you know that every day, I would try to lie beside you?" I raised my eyebrows in surprise. "I don't know why. I just liked the thought of me lying beside you. It's like you were a comfort to me just being there. I just can't explain it."

Now that she mentioned it, I remembered her always being near me during those naptimes. I told her this. "But I thought it was always *me* who was always trying to sleep next to *you*."

"Oh, really? Wow, I always thought it was just me trying to get close to you," she said, taking a sip of her tea. Then she laughed.

"What? What's so funny?"

"Now it all makes sense to me is what's funny," she said, covering her mouth with her hand the way girls do so others cannot see them laugh or smile.

"What makes sense?"

"'Oh Elizabeth. Do you think that I could have a little kiss?' Remember how in kindergarten you would always come up to me at the end of the day and ask for a little kiss?" I nodded. She kept giggling. "Now it makes sense to me. Of course, you would want to lie somewhere near me if you would also want a little smooch."

I started laughing too, just remembering how funny it was for little five-year-olds to have such grown-up thoughts and feelings. We just didn't know how mature those thoughts were at the time.

"What happened after that? Why did you stop doing stuff like that?"

It was a good question. I shrugged. "I guess that it's because of my general lack of success, and that we didn't have nap time anymore after kindergarten."

The waitress arrived with our dinner and laid it on the table. I thanked her, and she asked if everything was to our liking.

"Yes, thank you Irene. I think that we're good," I said, and she went to see how the people at the tables near us were doing. I unwrapped my silverware from the napkin, and Elizabeth did the same. "You first," I said, gesturing at the food.

She reached across the table, stuck a fork in the spaghetti. Swirled it around and took a bite.

"Mmm, that's good Lucas."

I thought it might be difficult for her to reach across the table for the entire meal to get food. With my long arms, it wouldn't be that much of a problem. I couldn't let her go through dinner this way.

I stood and walked around the table.

"What are you doing?" she asked.

"I decided I'd come sit next to you," I said, pulling out the chair beside her. "Don't you think makes sense if we were on the same side of the table?"

"Yeah, it does."

I sat down, and we poked at our meal for a few minutes in silence. I could feel her body next to mine in a way I had never felt before. It was like we were sitting closer together than ever before, but I know that we have sat close enough together for our thighs to be touching each other at other times in the past. This feels different.

"This is nice, Lucas. I like this," she said, reading my mind.

"Me too," I said, staring into her auburn eyes. From this close, I saw flecks of gold in her irises, making them seem more stunning than ever before. She reached down, grabbed my left arm, and put it over her shoulders, drawing us closer. I could feel the warmth emanating off her body.

"Lucas," she said, "you have the most striking blue eyes. Did anyone ever tell you that?" I shook my head no. I couldn't speak. My grandma told me that all the time, but it wasn't the time to bring that up. "Well, you do."

I smiled. Our faces were inches from each other. I could feel her warm breath puff against my face. This was the first time I could think of someone outside of my family paid me a compliment like that.

"Thank you for this evening," she said, but in a lower voice.

"You're welcome. But remember, it's not over yet," I reminded her.

"I know. I'm just thanking you now in case I forget later. Come on, our chicken is getting cold, and we have a movie time to make."

With our chicken finished, the plates cleared away, and the check and tip paid, I helped Elizabeth with getting her coat on. In the car, she held my hand all the way to the movie theater. The first, and to me, hardest part of the date was complete.

***

The second part of our date went well. I had my arm around her through most of the movie. It was the latest Nicholas Sparks flick. I lost all interest in the movie five minutes into the film. Elizabeth, however, seemed to enjoy it. She laughed occasionally, clutching my arm during some of the funniest moments. Then, during the expected emotional twist near the end of the film, she squeezed my arm tighter. Because I didn't pay much attention to the film, the meaning was lost on me. However, that's not to say I didn't enjoy the experience.

Just sitting in that little, dilapidated theater with her was enough to make the evening wonderful for me. I have never had that kind of experience before, where I was alone with a girl able to express any kind of affection towards her. Before now, I had not known what it felt like to share that kind of closeness with a girl. It was a very wonderful feeling.

The movie was over. We were alone in my dark car, on the way back to Elizabeth's home. I had the heater turned up full blast. There was a digital LED thermometer that read 30° on the side of the First National Bank of Nicholas County in Summersville. This made tonight the coldest night of the season so far. The time was just past ten-thirty, so we would make Elizabeth's curfew with no problems.

With the radio turned off, the only sounds in the car were the hum of tires moving across the cold pavement and the whirring sound of air blowing through the vents. Elizabeth seemed to be content with the silence. She had her hand in mine, resting on the center console between our seats. I was quiet because I just did not know what to say.

I felt like this had been as perfect an evening as I could have imagined. When I picked her up, I scored some points with her dad. I let her know how beautiful I thought she looked. At the restaurant, I made her feel special when I removed her coat. I managed not to make a fool out of myself during dinner. I thought the touch of moving over to sit beside her during dinner went over very well. Ashley would have approved. Then, the two hours sitting in the movie theater together were wonderful.

"What are you thinking about?" Elizabeth asked, breaking my reverie.

"You and me," I replied after a moment. "What about you? You're awfully quiet yourself."

I sensed her smile in the darkness.

"I've been thinking along those same lines." More quiet. "Lucas?"

"Yes?"

"I think that I really, really like you."

"That's what I've been thinking, too."

"What? That you really, really like yourself?" she said, amused.

"You know what I mean, Elizabeth," I smiled.

"Say that again."

"What?"

"My name."

"Elizabeth?"

"No, not like that. Say it like you did before," she explained.

I stared forward in the darkness for a second before I understood. Then, in the smoothest voice I could muster, said, "Oh, I've really enjoyed this evening, Elizabeth darling. You are ravaging and extraordinarily gorgeous."

Her face flushed. She laid a hand on her chest. "I don't think I've ever heard you say my name like that before. I like that," she purred.

"Thanks." I don't know where I pulled that from, but man, I felt awkward. I'm sure my friends would make fun of me for the rest of my life had they heard me say that. Then I thought, *"What were they doing tonight?"*

She said, "Okay, you asked me earlier this week. Now it's my turn to ask you. Where do we go from here?"

I was halfway expecting to hear this question tonight. I've spent some time thinking about what the answer should be. Much depended on how well the date went this evening. This was unexplored territory for me, and I wasn't sure what to say or what the next step was. I told her as much.

"I don't know about you, but I would like to spend some more time seeing you like this. Like tonight," she said. My heart skipped a beat. "I could get used to this. And if people see us spending time together, holding hands and stuff, and they ask me 'What? Is he your boyfriend or something?' I would tell them yes. Is that what you're looking for?"

"Very much so," I said in as calm a voice as I could, but inside, my heart was racing. "That would definitely fulfill a dream of mine."

"Me too," she agreed. "I had one of those schoolgirl crushes on you for the longest time. I feel the same way."

"Something else I've been thinking about, going along those same lines."

"What's that?"

"I've liked you for so long, and it's finally gotten to this point, and I've dreamed about getting together with you for so long. I don't want to screw anything up. If something is not working, or I'm doing some that you don't like or approve of, please tell me."

"Oh, Lucas," she laughed. "I can't think of anything that you do that I don't like or disapprove of. You're not like the other guys that only want to go out and get drunk on the weekends, always has a big chew of tobacco in their cheeks or gets all of us girls into their backseats trying to get our clothes off. You're different and always have been. That's why I like you so much."

"Thanks. I pride myself on being different."

"You're welcome," she said, squeezing my hand.

I made a left-hand turn onto Elizabeth's street.

"Thanks again," I said, "for making this an evening that I'll never forget. You were more wonderful that I imagined you could be. And I hope every time we do this, it'll be as good as it was tonight."

"You're welcome," she blushed, "you're not the only one who thinks that this date couldn't have turned out better.

I pulled into her driveway, parked the car, but left the engine running with the lights on. "Here we are," I said, looking out through the windshield.

"Here we are," she echoed.

Her house was mostly dark. Only the porch light and the lights shining through the blinds coming from her parents' bedroom were visible. They were no doubt waiting for their little girl to make it home safely.

She collected her pocketbook and gathered her coat for herself. "Lucas, again, I've had a really wonderful time tonight, and I very much want to do this again."

"Me too," I agreed. "Let me walk you to your door."

"No, you don't have to. It's too cold for me to ask you to do that. I'll be fine."

"Now, I'd feel the evening wasn't complete if I watched you get out of this car by yourself and go inside."

To prevent any further argument, I opened my door and got out of the car. I walked around to the front of the car where the headlights shined against my jacket. She met me at the front of the car and smiled up at me.

"Lucas, really, you didn't have to, but I appreciate it."

I offered her my arm, and she clutched it tightly. This was better than holding hands at this point because it let us share some of our body heat. We walked slowly, quietly to her front steps that way. The vapor of our breaths hung in the air. I heard dogs barking in the distance. The air smelled clean. Like a vent letting out the pleasant aroma of a dryer sheet.

When we arrived at the base of her steps, she let go of my arm and turned to face me. "Once again, thanks for this evening."

As she said this to me, I felt something cold land on my face. I brushed my hand across my face reflexively. I looked at my hand and didn't see anything. I looked at Elizabeth, and she was looking with a broad smile up into the night sky with her hands raised, palms up. As I looked at her, I saw snow falling around us. In the illumination from her porch light, it gave the effect that the snow was falling on her and her alone, making it a very exquisite thing to see.

"Look Lucas, snow!"

She looked beautiful as she said this. The emotions and circumstances of the evening swelled to this point. I couldn't help myself. I took a step forward, put my hands on her hips, and drew her towards me. She looked up at me in surprise, probably correctly thinking that I have done nothing like this before.

Then I kissed her. Her lips felt warm against mine. Her mouth opened slightly as her even warmer tongue darted into my mouth, causing my knees to go weak. Then she broke the kiss, leaned back with her arms around my waist and looked into my eyes.

"I've wanted to do that for a long time," I said, emitting a giggle.

"Me too." Her eyes twinkled in the porch light. "Good night, Lucas."

"Goodnight Elizabeth."

Without another word, she walked up the steps, opened the door, and left me standing alone. I collected my thoughts for about a minute, savoring all sixty seconds. I reached up and used a forefinger to wipe my lips dry. Only a few minutes had elapsed since I reached the landing. In those few minutes, my life changed. A first, a real first, just happened to me. That kiss was something that I would hold on to and remember for the rest of my life.

I did not even notice the heavily falling snow or the cold on my way home.

CHAPTER TWENTY-FIVE

While Lucas and Elizabeth were on their date, having a good time, Jake's evening was not going as well. As part of his punishment, he had to stay at home for the evening. Jake did not mind so much. It is not as if anyone asked him to do anything with them, anyway. He had heard about some big party somewhere in town, but they did not invite him. There had also been rumors that Lucas and Elizabeth had a date tonight.

This perturbed him somewhat. He thought he liked Elizabeth, and maybe that she liked him. He thought so because she sometimes seemed to flirt with him. She was about the hottest girl he had ever seen, and he wished she would pay attention to him.

It made him jealous, and he wondered how guys like Lucas did it. How what seems to be an average guy with an easygoing way somehow ended up getting the best girl, captain of the football, basketball teams, etc. Jake didn't know if Lucas realized it, but he had the respect of all his peers. When Lucas was at home healing his shoulder, Jake would hear his classmates talk about Lucas. From what Jake heard, most of their classmates looked up to Lucas.

Jake wanted that. He wanted to be the guy that had everything. He thought he had a personality girls would like if he just had an opportunity to show them. People had told him he looked like the late Paul Walker, the guy known for the *Fast and the Furious* movies. Jake knew girls thought he was a good-looking guy. He just could not understand why the girls were not flocking to him.

Well, he had some idea, and it all had to do with the medication he had to take. He knew that whatever pills his parents were making him take suppressed his personality. His parents got very upset if he did not take the pills. Sometimes he felt like a sweet red sports car with no engine. It looks great but does nothing.

This evening, his parents rented some kind of romance movie that his mom had wanted to see. Jake had no particular interest in the movie. Meanwhile, with his parents curled up on the couch together, watching the movie, Jake spent the evening locked up in his room playing a mindless alien blasting video game on his X-Box. Jake's parents were strict about what he could and could not do, but at least they paid little attention to the video games he played. He especially loved to play the shooting games. His opinion was the gorier the game, the better. He could sit in his room for an entire day and play nothing but games like these. He received some sort of personal satisfaction every time he blasted some bug-eyed monster to bits.

Jake had been in this town now for about a month, and no one had asked him to do anything with them. He knew he did not get off to a good start after sending Lucas to the hospital on his first day of school. He apologized to Lucas for doing it. He did not know what more these people wanted from him. He thought the apology would be enough.

Then, when he made a few friends, the thing happened in gym class. He noticed in his return to school following his suspension that a few of the people that he considered his friend stopped talking to him. He knew it was because he tackled Hunter without provocation, but they did not know how Hunter had been treating him. How he had been teasing Jake in the locker room for being new. Jake hoped Hunter had learned his lesson.

As long as he had to take these pills, he knew he would not be his true self. If he could fully let his personality show, he knew he could get all kinds of friends and girls.

He thought about all of this while he blasted aliens: the pills, his lack of friends, his developing a crush on Elizabeth, and therefore some slight jealousy towards Lucas. It should have been him out on that date tonight with Elizabeth. If only there was a way to stop taking those pills without his parents finding out about it.

On the TV screen, some green, bug-eyed alien blasted him to death with a gun that shot out green slime. He took the break in the action to look around his room.

His parents had painted his wall a depressing, light blue color. They said that the color was supposed to help him sleep. He was not sure it worked, but it was still depressing, nonetheless. He had a closet where he kept his shirts and other junk. There was a five-drawer dresser in one corner containing his pants, socks, and undergarments. He had pictures of his grandparents and a few relatives on top of the dresser. His television stand held a nineteen-inch television on top of it, with an X-Box game system and about twenty different shoot-'em-up games stowed underneath. He had a nightstand beside his bed that had an alarm clock and an ugly lamp resting on top. His bed had a light green comforter on top of it, contrasting nicely with his walls. Jake failed to notice the aesthetic value of the colors of his room. Underneath the bedspread were the matching sheets his mom had just washed today. Jake had to put them on the barren mattress after he got home from school.

His mom stayed at home. She made sure their house stayed neat and clean. However, she wasn't Jake's maid. It was his responsibility to make his bed, fold and put away his clothes.

In fact, now that he thought about it, his parents never really touched his bed.

Then, like a match struck in a dark cave in the recesses of Jake's mind, he got an idea.

CHAPTER TWENTY-SIX

I woke up on Saturday morning to find a nice white blanket of snow had settled on the ground overnight. Amazingly, I slept soundly through the night. After I got home from the date, I had to play 'twenty questions' about the date with my family. I was still wound up after the grilling ended. I thought sleep would be impossible, but thankfully, that was not the case.

I slept like a baby.

Since it snowed, the weekend was ruined. It used to be that when it snowed, I could not wait to get out and go sleigh riding. Now that I am older, I don't get as excited about that kind of stuff anymore. I would rather stay inside and play video games or read a book.

Our county is very good at getting roads plowed and salted when it snowed or iced. With this being the first snow of the year, the Department of Highways did not get all the roads cleared as fast as they do later on in the winter. By the time they got my road scraped and cleared of snow, it was Sunday afternoon and too late to go out and do anything.

I spent my weekend doing homework, reading a book, playing video games with Blake, and thinking about Elizabeth. I also had a few friendly phone calls with her. I did not talk to any of my other friends.

When speaking to Elizabeth, we talked about our date, and about school, and about pretty much everything, except where our relationship was headed. We agreed to take it slow, and if our phone calls were any sign, then we were going to be going at a snail's pace. The kiss on our first date may seem like moving fast to most people, but I thought of it more as a check to see how compatible we were.

If the kiss were any sign, I would say we were extremely compatible. That's just my opinion, though.

When we woke on Monday for school, all the snow had melted, and the roads were clear. I went without wearing the sling on my shoulder for much of the weekend, but I still wore it today. My shoulder seemed to be feeling much better, though. I could see progress.

I was a little late getting ready as usual for school, and by the time that I walked outside to my car, Blake, Allen, and Brian were standing by my car looking at me with their arms crossed. It almost looked like they were trying to intimidate me.

I stopped before reaching my car. "What's up guys? You ready to go?" They looked at me in stone icy silence for a few moments. "What's the problem?"

"You screwed up our evening," Brian said. "We didn't appreciate you not being there on Friday night."

"What can I say? I was busy," I explained. "Besides, I thought you were going to a party."

"Well, I didn't," Brian said.

"We know you were busy," Allen said, "but that's not a good enough excuse."

"Aw, come on guys," I laughed. "You know what I was doing, and all of you wished that you could have been in my place. And I see by the looks on your faces that I'm right. It was the first date that I have ever had, so don't you guys make me feel guilty because I didn't hang out with you all? So, what's the problem?"

It annoyed me they were giving me the third degree.

"We didn't have a fourth for Madden," Allen said. "I had to play on a team by myself while knuckleheads one and two here," gesturing at Blake and Brian, "kicked my butt all night long. At least if you would have been there, I would have had a fighting chance!"

I recognized they were just playing with me, but I also knew that the most mundane of things would get Allen worked up. I thought it was funny that this was what they argued over. It is also sad. However, they were my friends. That was why it didn't bother me so much. They were just trying to bust my chops.

"Come on you guys," I said, unlocking the car, "we're running late. I'll tell all the juicy details that I couldn't tell Blake with my family around. Get in the car."

This got a little cheer from everyone, but left Blake confused. We picked up Stone and he gave us all the juicy details of the party that he went to on Friday. He said that the party was so good, that it did not break until sometime Saturday afternoon. I have always known Stone to be a big party animal, and it would not have surprised me if he was the reason that the party lasted for so long.

He asked about my date too, but I was vague with the details. I would talk to anyone in this car about pretty much anything, Blake excluded, but there are parts of my life that I would rather they stay in the dark about.

No one remembered to call me out for not delivering the spicier details of my date.

Besides, I was sure that by lunch, they would all be able to piece together what happened through the gossip that was sure to have spread through the school by second period.

CHAPTER TWENTY-SEVEN

During homeroom, I did not do too much talking to anyone. The mood in the room was somber. Everyone had a case of the Mondays. I bid Elizabeth and Ashley a good morning and said hello to anyone else that I cared to speak with. I just wanted to skip everyone's interrogation about my date, so I thought silence was the best policy.

I noticed something about Jake that seemed to be a little different this morning. He seemed to be dressed a little nicer today, in some khakis and a burgundy polo shirt. This contrasted with his usual attire of black pants, black t-shirt, black shoes.

He was in his usual seat in front of Elizabeth and Ashley. He was not really talking to anyone. He was just sitting there with a little self-satisfied grin on his face. I do not think that I have seen him smile much before in the couple of months that he has lived here. I have seen him smile when someone said something funny, but I have never seen him have an extemporaneous smile on his face. Maybe he decided that the Jake he had been was not cutting it at his new school, and he decided to change a to fit in better with his new environment. He could just be playing a wolf in sheep's clothing. I don't know.

When the bell rang at the end of the period, I walked over to Elizabeth while she collected her books. "Hey,"

She collected her last book and then turned to face me. "Hey there yourself," she said with a smile on her face, "I was wandering something . . ."

"What's that?"

"I was wondering if maybe you could come over and help me with my homework tonight."

Before I could answer, someone bumped into my bad shoulder, sending a shooting pain down my arm.

"Oww! What the heck!" I grabbed my shoulder and spun around to see who it was, but there was no one left in the room. All I could see was Jake's back, hurrying away from us.

It didn't seem a random coincidence. He sits in front of Elizabeth, closer to the doorway where a person would normally get up and go straight out of the room. This was no accidental bump. For Jake to bump me from behind, he would have had to get up from his desk, go to the back of the classroom away from the doorway, and circle around to be walking in the direction he was walking when he bumped into me. It had to have been premeditated, but I wondered why.

I was rubbing my shoulder when Elizabeth echoed my thoughts. "What a jerk. I wonder what his problem is."

"I don't know," I said. "Though I have my suspicions that it involves the beautiful girl standing in front of me. I can tell from how he looks at you he likes you." She smiled, embarrassed. That kind of thing is a normal part of life for someone like Elizabeth. "I wonder if he's on drugs."

Elizabeth agreed. "I mean, when he first moved here a couple of months ago, he seemed like a pretty nice guy. Now suddenly he gets into a fight, which you say he had no reason for getting in to begin with. He's been giving you dirty looks in class, and now he bumps into you like that without apologizing. What a jerk! Yeah, maybe you're right. Maybe he is on drugs."

"I don't know what his problem is. But I think there is something wrong with him. From what I've seen since he has been here, it seems he has a bit of a violent streak. I wonder if there's any way to see all the places that he has been before he came here. Maybe he has a criminal record or something. If he does, then maybe we could figure out if there's something wrong with him. Maybe we could Google him or something. See what comes up." I don't like to be nosy, but this guy seemed like trouble.

She wrinkled her nose. "Wouldn't that be kind of nosy? I don't know if I would be comfortable with someone doing that to me without my knowing."

"Yeah, but this is different."

"How so?"

"With you," I pointed out. "there's nothing to be suspicious about. You're just a normal, but beautiful, teenager. With him, we know he has moved around a lot. Or so he says. And we know he has displayed some violent tendencies by busting me up, and for starting that fight in gym class last week. I would say for our own peace of mind, that's enough to warrant an investigation into his past if we can. But who knows, we may come up with zilch."

"I don't know," she hesitated, "let me think about it before you do anything. And if you do anything, I want to be there when you do it."

"Ok, think about it. But I think we should. But yes, I'll come over and help you with your homework this evening. Is there going to be any homework?"

"I don't care," she said. "It's just an excuse for you to come over."

"Sounds good to me."

Mrs. Gibson came up to us and said, "Ok, lovebirds, move it along, or you're going to be late for class." Word must have traveled fast if Mrs. Gibson knew about us already.

"Yes, Mrs. Gibson," we replied in unison.

***

I had not had the chance to talk to Ashley over the weekend, so during gym class, I cornered her and asked if she had talked to Elizabeth since our date.

"Lucas, I've never seen her this way before. With every other guy that she has been out with before, she acts like she does it just to be going out, or doing it because that she feels that, as a cheerleader, she has to be dating someone. You know what I'm saying?"

I nodded my head, even though I did not understand the whole being a cheerleader and being popular thing. I have my friends I hang out with and my sports I play, but I do not really care about what other people say or think about me. Except for the people who are my friends. Their opinions are the only ones that matter to me.

"But, when I was over at her house yesterday after the roads finally got cleared off," she continued, "the way she described the date and the way she felt about what happened differed from any other time. I don't know all the details, but I would say you're on the right track with her."

"Did she tell you about the end of the date?"

I was oblivious to everything happening in the gym. Basketballs bounced. Whistles blew. Sneakers squeaked. All of that was secondary to what was on my mind right now. Ashley let on that Elizabeth did not tell her everything about our date. Let's see if she relayed this little tidbit of information.

"What about it? What? Did you two kiss or something?" When I did not answer her, she exclaimed, "Oh my god! You kissed her!"

I looked around and saw several people turn in our direction. I turned back to her still disbelieving face. "Keep it down a little," I told her in a soft tone, hoping that she would notice the level of my voice, and keep hers on that level.

"Sorry," she said, softer this time. She looked down. Bit a fingernail, thinking about something. She shook her head. "Lucas, I can't remember a time where she has done that before."

"Done what?"

"Kissed a guy on a first date. That's a rule of hers." She paused. Shook her head with her eyes downcast. "Excuse me."

With that, she turned and ran through the gym doors leading to the locker room hallway. One door swung for a few seconds before coming to rest.

Coach Nixon must have heard Ashley's outburst, and then saw her run out of the gym. He came over to see what the problem was.

"Come on Lucas, what did you do? Is she okay? You didn't make her cry, did you?"

I looked at the still swinging gym doors. "I don't know what got into her, Coach. We were talking about something that happened over the weekend, and then she got upset about something and left. I don't know what the deal is."

"Was it something bad that happened?" he asked, interested. He liked to know what was going on with his students outside of the school confines. That way, he could keep an eye out for anything unusual.

"No, I was telling her about a date that I had on Friday night. That's all."

He smiled. All the coaches in our school seemed to be aware of the relationships their athletes had. I bet he knew I had not been out on any dates before, or maybe he had already heard about my date. "Hmm, maybe you had better go check on her."

"Coach, she's probably in the girl's locker room right now," I pointed out. "I can't go in there."

Coach Nixon took a quick glance around the gym and then turned to me. "Sure, you can. There's no one in there. I'll go stand watch and keep any girls from going in there while you do your thing."

I did not know that I had quite this level of trust coming from him, but I guess that if you are a teacher's aide, that implies some level of trust. After all, he had to approve of me to the principal for me to get this position.

A thought occurred to me. "But what if she's…you know, in a state of undress?"

He laughed. "Knock on the door and ask her before you go barging in."

We went out into the hallway where the locker rooms were, and he took up a position beside the girl's locker room door. "Go ahead. Give it a knock. The last thing that I need is some girl crying in my gym class. Don't repeat that," he said, shaking his finger.

I nodded, scared to death. On the one hand, I have never been in the girls' locker room. It is supposed to be holy ground. You hear rumors and descriptions of it, but you never know until you actually see it. The boys' locker room was like a dank, dark dungeon, and all the smells that one would assume were associated with a damp, dark dungeon. But with the girls' locker room, you hear stories. Such as, they have leather seats in there for the girls to relax in before and after class. You also hear that they have a nice hot tub, which every guy in the school would love to know if that was true or not. Our locker room has a hot tub that looks like an oversized metal bucket with an outboard motor attached to stir up bubbles.

Every guy would want to know where the locker area was at in relation to the boys' locker room, so that a hole could be properly drilled. You also hear tales of bright colors, pinks, blues, reds, all over their locker room.

I knocked on the door and asked her if she was decent. I heard a sniffle, and then a vague, "Yes."

My first impression upon entering the locker room is that all myths about the girls' locker room are, in fact, just myths.

It is almost exactly like the boys' locker room, just an opposite floor plan. The faint smell of baby powder floated in the air. The showers were the first thing you came to after entering, and then next you come to the locker/changing area. The lockers run ten deep along three walls in the back corner of the locker room. They are six feet tall and painted orange. Neither of our school colors included orange. They are gold and blue. There were wooden benches arranged like a big U, running alongside the three locker walls.

This was where I found Ashley, sitting with her back to me, in the very back corner of the locker room. Her face was buried in her hands. I walked over to where she was sitting and sat down beside her.

"Ashley, are you okay?" I asked quietly, although my deep voice still bounced off the dank walls.

The reply that I got was lost among her sobbing. I put my arm around her to, hopefully, give her some comfort. I did not know what I was comforting her for, but this is what I feel like I needed to do. To my surprise, she wrapped both of her arms around my stomach and set her head on my shoulder.

She continued to cry as I rubbed her back. "There, there Ashley. It will be okay. Just tell me what's the matter. We can talk about it. You know you can tell me anything."

She lifted her head from my shoulder and looked at me, with a tear running down her cheek that she wiped away with the back of her hand. She gave a sad smile and laughed. "You're just not bright sometimes. You know, Lucas?"

I opened my mouth to say something, but she stopped me.

"I didn't mean that. I'm sorry."

I nodded my head that I understood.

"Lucas, did you ever wonder why I like to do stuff with you, why I call you on the phone probably more than I do anyone else, or why I'm always willing to listen to you talk about Elizabeth or anything else that's on your mind? Do you ever wonder, Lucas, why for the past year or so, I haven't been dating anyone? And do you really need for me to tell you what is wrong with me after telling me about your first big date with anyone, much less my best friend?"

And like an anvil being dropped on my head, it hit me.

She was right. I *am* so stupid and blind. She did not need to tell me any of this. Had I taken the time to think about my good friend Ashley, I would have already known the answers to her questions, or at least guessed. If my focus had not been on Elizabeth for these years, I should have known how she felt. Upon this, a thought occurred to me.

"Ashley, do you remember a while back, when I was really talking to you a lot, and when I was calling you all the time, and you were dating Jeff at the time?" I said. She nodded her head, the corners of her eyes still glistening with tears. "It was then that I would have liked to have pursued a relationship with you. I don't know if it was jealousy or what. But when it looked like you and Jeff was getting serious, and you didn't really want to talk to me much at the time because of Jeff, I moved back to having my little crush on Elizabeth."

I saw the lights come on behind her eyes. "Oh, my goodness, that's what all of *that* was about?" she asked, breathless.

I gave her a blank look. I couldn't think of a way to answer her. We sat on the hard bench in silence. We had to let that revelation sink in. I comforted her while her tears continued to flow. It was all that I knew to do.

I heard the locker room door crack open. Coach Nixon stuck his head in the door and swiftly ducked back out. "Lucas, you'd better come on out here. I'm going to have to get the girls in here to change before the bell rings, and if I don't do it soon, I'm going to have a lot of teachers very mad at me for making these girls late."

"Okay, Coach!" I called to the receding head.

I couldn't remember a time when I had to talk to a girl in this state, much less one of my best friends. It seemed like she was mad at me, but then again, maybe she was also disappointed in something. I didn't know how to read girls when they were in this emotional state. Well, any emotional state, really.

Through all of this, something else occurred to me. "Ashley, if this is making you this way, then why did you try to get us together?"

She shook her head and wiped a tear away before answering. "That was the hardest thing that I have ever done."

"But why did you do it?"

Again, a shake of the head, but this time with a smile. "All that I want is for you to be happy, and I knew that for as long you had your crush on her that *that* was what you wanted to be happy. I was tired of seeing you look at her with those puppy dog eyes and her pretending not to notice you. So, while Elizabeth and I were talking during lunch one day—before you came back—about you, I realized what I had to do."

With Ashley telling me her side of things, I realized what a huge sacrifice she had been making all this time. I didn't know if

I could have remained as close of friends over the years with the three of us had I been in her shoes. I have, and have had feelings for her, but just not on the level of the feelings I have had for Elizabeth.

Historically, Ashley and I get along better than Elizabeth and myself. With Elizabeth, finding common ground for a conversation having nothing to do with school would sometimes be difficult to find. Ashley and I have never had any problems finding things to talk about. We always seemed to have more in common. I just put Elizabeth in an entirely different category over the years.

That might have been unfair to Ashley, but I hoped she hadn't reached her breaking point. With that thought, I dared to ask, "I don't know what to say, Ashley. What are we going to do now?"

She wiped her nose with the back of her sleeve after pulling back from me. "I don't know either, Lucas. We need to talk somewhere when we have some time to get some things out on the table. But I don't know if I can do it anytime soon. It's been tough being this close to you, knowing that you liked my best friend the whole time. I mean, I had to support you in it. I didn't know what else I could do," she said, throwing her arms up in exasperation.

"I know. I need to think as well, but I don't think that I can break things off with Elizabeth. And I don't want to lose you as a friend, that's for sure."

"That's just it Lucas. I'm not sure if I can be yours and Elizabeth's friend right now, if I feel the way I do about you."

I didn't know how to answer that. Nor did I have time to think up a response.

I heard an urgent "Lucas!" come from the direction of the door. I stood up and looked down at Ashley. She had a pleading look on her face.

It broke my heart.

"Sorry," I apologized, and ran towards the door.

As I left, I could hear even heavier crying coming from the back corner of the locker room.

***

In my biology class, we had moved from covering photosynthesis to learning about the ecosystem of a typical pond. I paid just enough attention to bluff my way through our typical not-so-pop quiz tomorrow. In this class, I caught on quickly to the fact that most of the info on the not-so-pop-quizzes usually ended up on the end of the chapter test. Therefore, all that a person had to do was memorize the questions from the quiz to get a good test score at the end of the chapter.

This was an excellent class to do some heavy thinking in if a person had any heavy thinking to do. It is also an excellent class to doodle in as well. This is some good information to know if you find yourself enrolled in one of Coach Wheeler's science classes.

I wondered what Ashley was going through over the weekend, or for just the past week, knowing that Elizabeth and I were going to have an actual date. Knowing what I had just learned from Ashley, I would say that it was not a good time for a little snowstorm to come through and keep her trapped at home for most of the weekend.

I felt for her, yes, but I did not know what I could do to make her feel better. I mean, I tried to give her a chance a year ago, but the timing was not right for her either. It's not as though you can go to a clothing store one week, see something on sale, and then pass it up. Later, you think about just how much you wanted that article of clothing. Then you go back to the same store the next weekend when it is not on sale, realize that you missed a good deal, and ask the clerk if you can have it at the last weeks' sale price. The answer is always 'no.'

Life just doesn't work that way.

I didn't know what was going to happen with Ashley's friendship and mine or even about her friendship with Elizabeth. If you think Ashley and I were close friends, those two have an even closer bond. They are almost like sisters. They would do anything for each other. They share each other's clothes. They go to the same places on the weekends. They stay at each other's houses all the time. I can imagine the strain this would put on their relationship.

This raised another question in my mind: did Elizabeth even know anything about this? To my knowledge, she didn't. I based this upon how she reacted the night Ashley told us how each other felt for each other. I still can't imagine what Ashley must have been thinking or feeling that night. It must have been extremely difficult for her to do that, knowing that she may throw away a chance for a relationship with me in the process.

That's the type of sacrifice you had to respect, and this hit close to home.

Now I needed to figure out what, if anything, I was going to say to Elizabeth about this. I did not even know if I should say anything, because I didn't want to add any gasoline to the fire their relationship may turn to in the near future.

After biology class ended, I was sitting at lunch with Elizabeth. Between bites of her lunch, she looked up, and then looked around the table. "Hey, has anyone seen Ashley? I haven't seen her since homeroom."

I kept silent.

"Yeah," one girl, Becky, on the other side of the table, responded, "I think I saw her leaving during last period. Her mom came and picked her up."

I knew Becky was an office aide during her second period class, so she may have been up front near the front doors to see this.

Elizabeth looked at her for a moment. "Oh, ok. Maybe she was sick or something," she said to me, returning to her meal. I hoped she would not remember that Ashley and I had the same first period class. She remembered. "Lucas, did you see her in your gym class?"

"Yeah," I hesitated and then "I saw her taking part in whatever they were doing. At one point, I saw her run into the locker room during class."

"Oh, well, that makes sense," Elizabeth said. "I think she's been having some stomach problems lately. That could be it."

I really didn't want to tell Elizabeth what Ashley told me in the locker room right now. I for sure don't want anyone knowing I was in the girl's locker room to begin with.

I spent the rest of the lunch period with Elizabeth, avoiding the subject of Ashley. It was a simple thing to do. I avoided this by making plans with Elizabeth for something to do this upcoming Friday night. She focused so much on the planning that she forgot about Ashley.

CHAPTER TWENTY-EIGHT

While Lucas would not admit to knowing anything about what was wrong with Ashley, Jake could tell anyone that asked him what was wrong with her. He *knew.* However, he would tell no one for the time being. Not that he had too many people to tell, anyway. A plan was forming in his head and that information could be a key to his plan.

Jake and Ashley had their second period English class together. What Elizabeth and Lucas did not know is that Jake sat right behind Ashley in that class. Therefore, when Ashley came in, sat down, and put her head on her desk, Jake immediately could tell that something was wrong.

He had paid little attention to Ashley so far. His focus had been mainly on watching Elizabeth. He knew that she rarely acted this way. She was usually bright, ebullient, and chatty, though she was not chatty so much with Jake. Before now, he had been in his own little world most of the time. Today, Jake could sense that there was something wrong with Ashley.

When she came in and put her head down, Jake noticed that the people that she usually speaks to were pretending not to pay any attention to her. *Some friends,* Jake thought, *you go through a hard time, and everyone abandons you.*

Seeing that no one was watching him, he reached up and rested his hand on Ashley's shoulder. She was startled, but said nothing.

"Hey," Jake whispered tentatively. "Are you okay?"

"Yeah," Ashley said, turning and wiping her nose on her sleeve. Jake removed his hand from her shoulder. He could tell that this was a lie. She smiled; her eyes cast downward. "Thanks for asking," she said, touching his hand. She then turned around and put her head back on her desk.

Jake did not take this as a dismissal. He leaned forward and whispered over her shoulder, "Is there anything that you want to talk about? You can tell me. I don't know anyone. Who am I going to tell?"

He thought that she may have giggled a little nasally giggle.

She picked her head up and again turned around slowly. She looked him in the eyes. Jake thought she had been crying. Jake did not know what she thought of him. From the impression that he had gotten from her over his first month here, he thought maybe she did not like him so much, or maybe she just did not know him well enough yet to talk to him very much.

Jake thought that as she was searching his face that she might have been measuring whether she could trust him. He also noticed that she possessed a nice set of green eyes.

She seemed to reach a conclusion. "Alright, but just as long as you promise not to tell anyone." Jake held his hand up in a little mock Boy Scout signal of trust. "I don't know if you know or not, but Elizabeth and Lucas went out on a date Friday night."

"I thought I heard that rumor."

"Now this is something that I have told no one before, so you got to keep it quiet," she said, looking him in the eye. He gave her a look that told her she could trust him. She leaned toward him and whispered in his ear, "I've had a big crush on Lucas for a while."

She leaned back. Jake had his raised his eyebrows, wondering why she told him this. Maybe she figured it was safe to tell him about it. If he told anyone about what she just said, then the people may think that he was lying, given the reputation that he had established. She probably knew that he did not have anyone to gossip to, anyway.

He would have never guessed that Ashley liked Lucas. A blind person could see the affection that Lucas had toward Elizabeth, but never would he have guessed that Ashley had the same feelings towards Lucas. Was this the reason for her breakdown?

"Ok, so what brought about your current state?" Jake asked thoughtfully.

Ashley told him of the confrontation that she had with Lucas a few minutes ago in gym class. She had gotten to where she had to run into the locker room when the bell rung, and the teacher came in and called for everyone's attention.

"I'll tell you more about it later," Ashley told him, and turned around.

This excited Jake. Not very many people up to this point wanted to talk to him much, but here was someone who did. Not only that, but she was pretty to go along with it.

That 'later' that she had mentioned did not come right away. As class went on, the teacher took notice that Ashley was not herself. Eventually Ashley told her she was not feeling well and wished to go call her mom to come and pick her up. The teacher trusted Ashley to ensure that she was not faking sick and sent her to the office to call her mom.

Ashley collected her books, got up, and walked quietly out of the room, leaving Jake to wonder about the rest of her story.

Jake wondered what could have happened in that locker room to cause Ashley's sorrow. Now that he knew for sure that Lucas and Elizabeth were now a quasi-item, it made him just that much more jealous. He knew that right now was not the time to do anything about it. He would bide his time. The plan that he was working on would take some time to complete.

He had to have Elizabeth. He thought she was the most beautiful thing that he had ever seen.

***

As the morning wore on, people noticed changes in Jake.

Jake was more alive, more vibrant than he had in a long, long time. You could see it in his posture. He was no longer walking around with drooping shoulders. You could hear it in his speech. He no longer responded to the teachers and fellow students under his breath. They no longer kept having him repeat himself. His voice was richer, fuller. If he was speaking to you, you could feel a change. He spoke to you as if he suddenly cared about what you had to say to him, and you could tell by the look in his eyes. His eyes no longer seemed glazed over, but they were now a more brilliant blue, fuller of life.

Inwardly, Jake was thinking a little more clearly. He was aware of a lot more than he had been before. He could see how people tried to keep their distance from him. He knew that how he acted before, and how he treated others, would not make him popular. He had to talk to people, get to know some of his other classmates better.

Today, it worked. Jake hoped that after his interactions with some of his classmates that they would see him in a different light. He hoped they felt like maybe he was an all-right guy after all the hoopla that surrounded his first couple of weeks of school. He also hoped that they could at least tell that he was trying.

First on Jake's mind was what the rest of Ashley's story was, and what he could find out about Elizabeth from her.

***

Jake made a bold move that evening. He knew where Ashley lived. He passed her house in the mornings on his way to school, and in the evenings, he sometimes saw her in her front yard playing with a little white dog.

Jake took on the pretense of seeing if Ashley was feeling better and go up to her house and see her. He had to walk to her house, as his parents did not allow him to have his driver's license yet. It was only a mile or so from his new home, and it was a chilly evening. Jake put on his heavy jacket and walked the distance to her house with his hands in his pockets.

As he approached her house, he saw her sitting with her little dog in her lap on her front steps. He walked across the lawn, and she did not notice Jake approaching until his long evening shadow cast over her. She looked up and had to shade her eyes from the setting sun.

"Hey," she said. "I'm surprised to see you here."

"You're about as surprised as I am, too," he said. "How are you doing?"

She stood up, dusting her backside off with one hand while holding the dog in the other. "Better, I think," she responded. "What brought you up this way?"

"To be honest with you, I'm not sure," he lied. "I kind of wanted to hear the rest of your story. It just seemed to me that something bad happened to you this morning, and I didn't think that any of your other friends noticed."

"Well, thanks," she responded. She then muttered something under her breath, which Jake did not quite make out but thought that it sounded something like, 'some friends.' Jake smiled. "Do you want to come in out of the cold here? You've got to be cold after walking all the way from your house."

"You know where I live?" he asked.

"It's a small community. Everybody knows where everyone lives, even the new people in town. People especially take notice when someone builds a brand-new house. I guarantee you that most everyone in Mt. Lookout at some point drove by your home to see what was going up. I know that my family did. Come on," she said with a laugh, holding the door open. "I'll make you some hot chocolate."

"How can I pass that up?" Jake said, going in the door first. Ashley closed the door behind her and released her little dog on the floor. He ran off somewhere into the back of the house.

Ashley's house had an immense living room. It was complete with leather furniture, a big-screen television. The room had surround-sound speakers arrayed around the room in between the mounted animal heads.

It was hard not to notice the animal heads. They were everywhere. Jake counted four stuffed deer heads, two large, mounted fish, and the centerpiece was a grizzly bear's head mounted right above the fireplace in the corner. Guessing correctly that Ashley's dad must have been an avid hunter, it did not surprise him to see a well-stocked gun cabinet up against one wall in between two of the deer heads. He made a mental note.

"Go on now," she told the little dog.

"What's his name?" Jake asked, gesturing at the dog.

"Snowball. Original huh?" she laughed. "He's a Maltese."

Jake raised his eyebrows as if that meant something to him. The fact was, Jake hated dogs, but he wouldn't tell that to Ashley.

"Come on in here," Ashley said, leading him into a well-appointed kitchen. "Have a seat over there at the table. My mom is in the den on the other side of the house. We'll stay in here so as not to disturb her local news on television."

Jake took the seat that Ashley had pointed him to, while Ashley put some water in a kettle and set it on the stove. She came to the table, pulled out a seat, and sat across from him.

"Thank you for this morning," Ashley said.

"Oh, it's nothing," Jake slapped the comment aside. "I don't like seeing people upset."

"Believe me, I don't like being upset. I try not to get that way. I especially try not to get that way at school," she said, shaking her head.

"If I recall correctly," Jake said, "you were in the middle of what happened this morning when class started."

Ashley looked at the ceiling silently for a moment, collecting her thoughts. The kettle whistled.

"Excuse me," she said, breaking out of her reverie.

She went and got some cocoa mix out of a cabinet beside the stove and put a heaping scoop in two empty mugs she had gotten out alongside the stove. She took a spoon and stirred the mixture that was in the two cups and then brought both mugs back over to where Jake was sitting.

"I hope you like marshmallows," she said, setting a steaming mug in front of him.

"Marshmallows are just fine," he said, taking a sip. He flinched as the cocoa burned his tongue. "Whew, that's still too hot."

Ashley was about to take a sip of hers when he said this. She heard his warning and set her mug down.

"Where were we this morning?" she asked.

"I think you had just run into the locker room when you had to stop telling your story."

"Oh, that's right," she said. She told him about Lucas coming into the girl's locker room, and ended with her telling Lucas that she could not see him while she still felt how she does about him.

She shook her head. "I don't know what I'm going to do. They've been my best friends since we were in elementary school together."

"I'll be your friend," Jake blurted. He couldn't believe those words fell out of his mouth, but somewhere in the back of his mind, a proverbial puzzle piece fell into place.

Ashley looked at him through the tears that had returned with the finishing of her story and smiled.

She sipped from her mug. "I think I would like that." They sipped their cocoa silently for a few minutes. "You're different from how I thought you would be. Since you've been here, you've given everyone the impression that you're mean or something. People think you might try to start a fight with them just for talking to you. But it seems, at least lately, that you're not that way at all."

Jake laughed. "I don't know whether to be offended or flattered."

He looked out the window to see that the sun had gone down. It was going to be another frosty night.

He had accomplished his goal for coming here this evening in trying to get some information about Elizabeth. He was really liking her and was trying to figure out a way to get her to talk to him. He thought that by learning more about her, he could figure out the best way to get her attention. It never occurred to him he would be abusing this newfound relationship with Ashley to do this.

"It's getting dark. I'd best be going home," he said.

"Oh, well, I can take you home if you want for me to," she said after they had finished talking more and finishing their cocoa.

"No, no," Jake said, rising from his chair. "I can walk it. It's not far, but I appreciate the offer, though."

"Are you sure?" Ashley asked, following him to the door.

"Yeah, it's no problem." He said, zipping up his jacket. "I'll see you tomorrow."

"Okay," she said, closing the door behind him.

Ashley wondered if she was making a mistake by talking to Jake. She knew what Lucas and Elizabeth thought about him, and that they were suspicious of him. However, from talking to him for the first time, she thought that maybe Lucas and Elizabeth were wrong. She suddenly realized that she did not care what Lucas and Elizabeth thought of her talking to Jake. He seemed OK to her.

***

As Jake walked down the side of the cold, dark road, he laughed aloud. He could not help but feel pleased at how this day had turned out. He went from having no friends to having just one. That didn't sound like much, but this one friend was an important friend to have.

Along his walk home, Jake took a slight detour. It was cold, but what Jake wanted to do for a few minutes would warm him up inside.

CHAPTER TWENTY-NINE

Starting the next day and over the course of the next week, I noticed a change in the dynamic of my friendship with Ashley. The first thing I noticed was that Ashley only talked to Elizabeth or me if she absolutely had to. She avoided us in the halls. She avoided us in the classrooms. She did not sit at our table during the lunch period anymore. Instead, she made a disappearing act during that time. All that I could get out of her, when I tried to say 'hello' to her, was a restrained smile.

I did not take her seriously when she told me she could not speak to us for as long as we were dating. I thought she might not want to talk to us as much, but I did not think she would completely cut off association with us either. I tried to put myself in her shoes. I could only imagine what she was going through right now. I would never think that she would just stop talking to us and treat us as though we were strangers.

Elizabeth told me that during the homeroom sessions, she still tries to strike up conversations with Ashley. However, Ashley just ignored her every time she tried. Elizabeth, after a week of the cold shoulder, eventually gave up hope of conversation.

While our relationship with Ashley almost dwindled to nothing, my relationship with Elizabeth was progressing very well. We talked together whenever we could, whether it was at home, school, or a restaurant. We talked on the phone every night, sometimes late into the night. We were getting to know each other very well. I was finding things out about her I never knew or guessed.

I learned things about her family. I did not know she had a great grandmother who was nearly one hundred years old and lived in Pittsburgh. She still got around well by herself. She could still walk to and from the market, which was near her home, which I think is amazing considering her age. I found out that her oldest brother had finally graduated from college last spring and had moved down to somewhere in Florida for a job at a TV station in Ft. Lauderdale. I found out her parents got married when they were both seventeen years old, which I believed had something to do with her older brother.

I learned some interesting things about Elizabeth. I found out that she was not very interested in going to college. Her parents strongly encouraged all their kids to seek post high school education. She wanted to go to the Vocational Center during her senior year and train to be a hairstylist. That way, whenever she graduated from high school, she would be well on her way to establishing a career.

She put it this way to me, "Everybody needs to get their hair cut, except for baldies like your dad."

She figured having a license to cut hair by the time that she was out of school would make it easier for her to leave home without having to rely on her parents to give her money to go to school. I pointed out that I carried the same genes as my dad does and may eventually someday go down that same path.

"That's okay," she replied. "You would still need to have someone cut your hair around the sides. But if I'm a hairstylist, I won't have to worry about trying to find a job, having time off in the evenings, or working on holidays. If I rent my own booth somewhere, then I can make up my own schedule."

I had to admit, it wasn't a bad idea. Unlike most kids our age, she had a plan. I couldn't say I had put as much thought into my future. I was leaning towards business management. That could change a hundred times before I left school. Graduation for us was still a couple of years in the future.

I learned she has never seen the ocean. This came as some shock to me. We have a large lake about ten minutes from our house with a nice little beach on it. She said that it satisfied her and her family with just going there and camping during the summers. I tried to explain the exhilaration that you feel to have waves crashing down over you or riding the waves into the shore on a little boogie-board. She did not see the excitement of waves crashing over her head every two minutes and nearly drowning her.

I learned little things about her that no one else knew. She told me she had a pineapple-shaped birthmark about two inches below and to the left of her belly button that no one outside of her family has ever seen. I tried to get her to show it to me, but to no avail. I told her I would have to see it to believe it. She still said no. I thought she was just trying to tease me.

I learned that when she was a little baby, she tried to climb out of her crib when her parents were not around. She fell and broke her little arm. Then, as soon as the arm healed, and the cast came off, she climbed out of the crib again and fell, but this time she did not break anything.

The more time that we spent with each other, the less nervous I was about being together. Before we got together, I got nervous every time that I tried to talk to her. She intimidated me. However, over these past couple of weeks, the more that we are together, the more comfortable I feel. It was much easier to have conversations and joke around with her without feeling as if she would be critical of everything that I said.

While everything was going great along those lines, the thing that was going on with Ashley was disturbing me very much. I saw her often hanging around Jake. I would see them walking together in the hallways, or sitting outside together during lunch. This solved the mystery of where she disappeared during lunch.

Not that I was worried about who Ashley hung around. She was her own woman and could decide for herself. Maybe she saw something in Jake she liked and was around him more and more, for whatever reason.

It was Jake that I was worried about being around her. My relationship with Jake was much the same as it was with Ashley right now: near total silence. Yeah, sure, now and then we will say 'hi' to each other in the halls or shoot some baskets with each other in gym class. Not that I minded.

I saw the way he looked at me whenever he saw me with Elizabeth. Or, I should say, the way he looked at Elizabeth when I was with her. He had this look in his eye that told me he had a thing for her. He didn't care if I was standing right there with her. He even looked at her that way whenever we saw him with Ashley. Ashley did not seem to know he was staring at Elizabeth, because she was busy trying to act as though she didn't notice us.

I do not see what those two have in common, so I wondered what they talked about . . .

CHAPTER THIRTY

"Ooo, Jake. Right there, oh, that's the spot." Ashley was not quite sure how she got to this point. Well, she knew how she got to *this* point, but that was not the point she was thinking about.

Jake and Ashley were on Ashley's bed in her bedroom. Ashley had the door cracked open because her parents told her to keep her door open while Jake was in here with her to prevent any fooling around.

That didn't deter Jake. He thought the television would have her parents' attention in the living room on the other side of the house, thinking that Jake and Ashley were in here studying. They could tell when a parent was approaching by the creaks in the old floorboards of Elizabeth's home. When that happened, they ceased making out and Jake retreated to the other side of the room where his book lay open on the floor, so it would look like he was studying.

Ashley's parents were deep into the Nightly World News, preparing for bed, and Jake was having a good time necking on Ashley. She was not getting the same enjoyment out of it that Jake was. She just made the right sounds and said the right things to make him think he was doing a good job. Ashley was thinking about different things entirely.

How did she get here? A month ago, she was one of the more popular girls in her class. She had no shortage of friends. In a month's time, all of that changed. After she confronted Lucas in the locker room, she decided she could not speak to him or Elizabeth for the time being. Maybe in the future, but right now, it was too tough on her seeing Lucas and Elizabeth together.

Her heart still ached for Lucas. She knew that was no one that she had ever met who she got along with better. She knew he knew her better than anyone else did, and she could confidently say she knew him better than anyone else did. Lucas would tell her things she knew he would tell none of his guy friends. She knew in her heart that he was a guy she could talk to about anything, and he would listen to her with an open mind and not ridicule her for what she had to say. He valued her thoughts and opinions like no one else did.

Lucas had had a crush on Elizabeth ever since Ashley could remember. At the beginning, it did not bother her. In fact, she thought it was cute of him having a crush on Elizabeth. Over the years, as the three of them grew together and gone through the grades, Elizabeth was the one who made more of a name for herself in the class. She was the one who had been head cheerleader until she quit the squad last month. Elizabeth was still active in the class government though, being the class vice-president for the past two years. That said something about being in a male dominated school that she could still earn an office of that stature. Elizabeth was someone everyone in the class knew at least something about because of what she did within the class.

Lucas and Ashley were a little different. Lucas played on the football and basketball teams, but truth be told, even though the coaches encouraged him to think about athletic scholarships after high school, he will probably never land one. He may get an academic scholarship, sure, but he is just not athletic enough to compete on the college level. The coaches kept encouraging him and whispering in his ear, so that he wouldn't lose his interest in sports.

Aside from playing sports, Lucas kept pretty much to himself. He limited his association to a close-knit group of friends he had around him since elementary school. He does not go to parties or go camping with the other guys on the weekends. He spent his time at home reading books or playing video games. He was just an average introverted high school kid, though he would never admit to it.

Ashley did not even have sports to add to her resume. She was in some of the advanced placement classes, and she did not take part in the class government or any sports. Lucas had his group of close-knit friends. Ashley didn't even have that. Lucas and Elizabeth had been her main two friends for much of her life, and now she does not even have them anymore. When she stopped being around Lucas and Elizabeth, all her other friends noticed, and when it came time to choose between Ashley and Elizabeth, everyone of course chose Elizabeth.

High school kids could be so cruel. It was all just one big popularity contest.

That was not Lucas and Elizabeth's doing, though. They tried to talk to Ashley, but she tried hard to ignore them. People at school thought Ashley, Lucas, and Elizabeth had a huge falling out of some sort, but nobody knew why. They thought because Elizabeth, and to a lesser degree, Lucas, are more popular, it must be Ashley who was in the wrong. So no one spoke much to her anymore, causing her to withdraw from others at school. She did not ask for this, but before she could do anything about it, it was too late.

One week, all was well with their little world. The next week, it came crashing down.

Ashley became friends with Jake, mainly because he was the one that was there for her when it all happened. She knew that Lucas and Elizabeth did not like Jake. She even knew why, but she could not imagine going through school alone, with no friends. When Jake started coming around after school, she did not deter him. When Jake started staying for dinner, her mom made extra food, and Ashley did not stop him. When Jake started making advances towards her, she thought only of her loneliness and did not dissuade him.

So here they were, at this point. Ashley lying on her back on her bed. Jake on top of her, kissing on her neck. Ashley was bored with it and decided that Jake had had enough fun for one evening.

She sat up quickly, shoving Jake aside. He looked at her in surprise. "What?" he asked when Ashley put a finger to her lips.

"I think I hear someone coming," she whispered.

Jake knew what to do. He immediately jumped off the bed and made his way over to the corner where his books lay. He was silent, looking at the open door for a moment.

"I don't hear anything," he said.

Ashley looked thoughtful for a moment. "I guess I was wrong."

He stood up and came back over to the bed. Ashley put a hand up and halted him. "No, no, I think we need to do something else now. It's getting late. I promise you'll get some another time."

She saw a flash of anger run across his face.

"Okay," he said, dejected, and sat back down.

She noticed this happening more and more with Jake. They would talk about something, then she would say something she thought was innocent, and he would give her an angry look. It worried her. With the pattern he established for himself since arriving in Mt. Lookout, she wasn't surprised. It was not as if he stayed angry or anything. He would give off little hot flashes, and then do what he was doing now: act as though nothing happened. Then sometimes she noticed he would be in a very good mood.

Ashley suspected that something was wrong with Jake. She looked over at him sitting in the corner. She thought he was a really an attractive guy. There had to be some reason he was sitting in her room right now. She thought he was out of her league.

Ashley knew other girls were a lot prettier than she was. She accepted this. She was given her lot in life, and she would have to play the hand life dealt her. She thought her nose was too large and she had too much acne. Maybe someday the acne will go away, and she will grow into her nose.

Her mother was like that. Ashley had seen pictures of her mom from when she was in school, and she had to admit that there was a striking similarity between the two of them. She had hope. Her mom used to get boyfriends easily if she so chose, and Ashley had never had very many problems getting a boy-friend, either.

"What are you thinking about?" Jake asked quietly from where he was sitting.

Ashley broke out of the reverie that she did not realize that she had been in. "Oh, nothing," she lied.

"You just looked like you were really thinking about something. I just wondered if it had to do with me."

"Maybe a little," Ashley said. "I was just thinking about what a guy like you is doing hanging around a girl like me." She smiled.

"I think it's because we both needed someone."

This hurt Ashley. Not because he said it, but because she knew it was true.

"But why Jake? I know why I don't currently have many friends. But you, you're different. When a person moves to a new town, usually the first thing that they seek is friendship. You're a good-looking, athletic guy. You shouldn't have any trouble making friends. But you've been here for three months, and I'm all that you seem to have. Why is that? I can understand a 'breaking in' period when you first moved here, but it seems like that you're different from the way you were when you first moved here."

"What do you mean?"

"Well, at first, you didn't talk to anyone. You were quiet most of the time," she explained. "The only time in class that you spoke was when the teacher asked you to answer a question that you didn't raise your hand for. Now, I hear you giving answers all the time in English class."

"Yeah."

"And now you don't seem like a robot anymore. It was, and maybe I just didn't notice this, like you never laughed or smiled. Maybe you did, but I never saw you. That's what I mean."

"There are reasons I acted that way."

"Now, it's my turn. What do you mean?"

He sighed. "A couple of years ago, I got really depressed and started doing some stuff."

Ashley had an aunt that was clinically depressed, so she could sympathize with Jake. She knew that depression could be a horrible thing, but she could not imagine being that depressed.

"I'm sorry to hear that," she said, patting the bed for him to come back over and have a seat so they could talk quieter. "What kind of stuff did you do?"

Jake took a moment to collect his thoughts, sighed, and then said candidly, "I vandalized some stuff."

"What did you do?"

"When we lived in Seattle," he began in a whisper.

This is the first time he mentioned living in Seattle. He had a deep voice that carried. Even though Ashley's parents had retired to their bedroom on the other side of the house, Jake did not want to chance waking them up.

"There was one night where I was really feeling bad about myself, and I got the idea that maybe breaking some stuff would make me feel better. I don't know why I thought that. So, after mom and dad went to bed that night, I sneaked out of the house. It was a cold, rainy night in the Pacific Northwest, but I didn't care. I went through some woods behind my house to get to the subdivision that ran behind us."

"Go on," Ashley said. This was interesting to her. She did not know where he was going, but she wanted to hear more.

"In this subdivision is where some of the upper middle-class families lived. They had nice two-story brick homes, complete with three-car garages and circular driveways. It was probably one in the morning at about this time," he shrugged. "When I got there, I didn't really have anything in mind specifically to do. The house that I had come out behind had a big plate-glass window on the back of the house looking out into the woods. I looked down at the ground and saw a couple of big rocks. I picked one of them up and heaved it through the big window."

Ashley giggled at this. "I'm sorry. I know that it's not funny. You broke their window?"

Jake shrugged again, smiling this time. "Why not? I didn't hear any alarms going off, so I ran off to another house and did the same to their bay windows. I think I hit two or three more houses before the cops showed up. I guess one house had a silent alarm. When the cops rounded the corner coming into the subdivision, I was standing in someone's front yard in mid-throw. Their lights hit me just in time to see this person's ornamental glass front door get demolished."

"What happened then?" Ashley asked, putting a hand over her mouth.

"The cops stopped their car, got out and yelled at me to 'freeze'. I knew I was busted, so I froze. When they yelled 'freeze', it's like it snapped me out of a trance. It wasn't until then that it occurred to me what I had been doing. I could have run. Both cops looked like they ate doughnuts for breakfast, lunch, and dinner. I could have easily outrun them, even though I was only like thirteen."

"Then what happened?"

"They hauled me down to the jail, called my parents, and locked me inside a jail cell. My parents showed up, talked to the cops. The cops let me go and my parents took me home."

"What did they say to you? Your parents."

"They told me I disappointed them in me. It was sinking in that I could be in big trouble, and I was feeling guilty about it. I had caused a lot of damage. I thought they were going to lock me away in juvenile hall."

She could tell that Jake was struggling with this. He was having a hard time getting the words out. "Did you?"

"No, my dad worked it out with the families. He paid for the damages and threw in an extra thousand dollars for their hardship for not pressing charges against me. They all went for it, so they let me off the hook."

"Your dad must have some deep pockets," Ashley stated.

"Yeah, his dad, my grandpa, was divorced and made a fortune in the stock market. When he died, since my dad was the only child, he left almost all the money to my dad."

This surprised Ashley. She knew Jake lived in a nice new house, but she did not know that Jake's family had any kind of money. She would have figured that if his dad were rich, they would have bought something like a mansion. She pointed this out to Jake.

He thought about it for a moment. "My dad's not like that. He doesn't like to show off his money. He doesn't believe in living a life of excess. That keeps him down to earth, and that is what I think makes him such a good man and father."

"He seems like a good guy," Ashley said.

"They were figuring out that something was wrong with me," he continued. "I didn't know what was wrong with me. I just knew that sometimes I was really depressed, even downright suicidal."

"I don't know what to say to that," Ashley said sympathetically, rubbing his arm.

"What's to say? One time, my parents caught me in the bathroom with my hand in a sink full of water and a plugged-in hair dryer. I was standing in front of the mirror, holding the hair dryer over the sink, trying to think of a reason to stay alive."

"Oh, my goodness," Ashley said, with both hands covering her mouth this time. "What did they do?"

"My dad rushed in and grabbed me, while my mom made a grab at the hair dryer. I don't remember much about what happened after that, except for crying in my mother's arms for most of the rest of the night." As the memory washed over him, he stared at the bed with his eyes misty. "I have never told that to anyone outside of my family except for my doctor."

Ashley gave him a deep hug. "I will never tell anyone," she vowed. "How old were you when this happened?"

"About the same age," Jake said. "This was like two months before I broke those windows. After I did that, they took me to a therapist."

"What did the therapist say?"

"They ran a bunch of tests on me. Asked me a bunch of questions. My parents said it was odd for me to behave this way.

They told him how I always seemed like such a happy kid. Then all the sudden I got depressed and they couldn't figure out why. When I got depressed, they didn't think much of it because I still had times when I was exceedingly happy. They asked my parents if anyone in our family had a history of mental disorders. On my mom's side of the family, she had some relatives that had had some problems. Then he diagnosed me with something called bipolar disorder."

"It sounds to me like you were just depressed." Ashley opined.

"I just told you about the depression and the suicidal episode that I had. I haven't told you that there were also times when I would get extremely hyper and happy. Sometimes I got so hyper that it made my nose bleed."

"Wow."

"Yeah, that's the thing with bipolar disorder. It's characterized by extreme mood shifts. One time you can be extremely happy, and then at other times you can get extremely depressed, even suicidal," he explained.

"What did they do?"

"What else do they do when they figure out that something is wrong with a person? They put me on some pills," he said, snorting in disgust.

"What kind of pills?"

"They put me on Lithium and Wellbutrin."

"Isn't Lithium the name of an old Nirvana song?" Ashley asked, trying to inject a touch of humor into the conversation. "Just kidding. What do those pills do for you or to you?"

Jake did not laugh at the sad joke. "Lithium keeps me from getting suicidal, but it makes me shaky sometimes. The

Wellbutrin keeps me from getting depressed, but it also made me act robotic."

"You're not on them anymore?" Ashley asked with her eyebrows furrowed in concern.

"No."

"Did the doctor tell you to go off of them?"

"No."

"Why did you quit them? Don't you need them?"

"I quit them because I was tired of not having any friends, and I thought that if I could be myself for a while, then maybe I could make some," Jake said, frustrated. "I know before I started having to take those pills, I had a lot of friends."

He looked up at her. "You're the only person who I have talked to in the past two or three years that seems to understand me even a little. But once people find out about my past, they don't want to have nothing to do with me. For that reason, I don't like to talk to people about my past."

"What caused your family to move here?" she asked, ignoring his remark.

He stood up and started pacing the side of the room that Ashley was sitting in. "After they diagnosed me with bipolar, my parents thought that maybe a change of scenery would do me some good. We moved from Seattle to El Paso."

Ashley's eyes widened. "Wow, that's a big move."

"I'll say. Our house in Seattle sold quickly. Dad could afford to sell it at a cheap price just so he could get rid of it. Then dad saw that his company had an office in El Paso, so he transferred there. I think that he just picked a random place on the map. We lived there for a while, and then we moved to Charlotte.

We were only there for a couple of months before we moved up here."

Ashley wondered if there was something behind the other moves after they left Seattle, but she would not push Jake to tell her anymore. She would not stop him if he told her more, though. He was staring at the floor. He stayed that way for nearly a minute. Ashley watched him, silent. It seemed to her like he was struggling with something.

She was starting to say something to break the silence when he seemed to come to a decision. He raised his head and looked at her.

"You have got to promise me that this doesn't leave these walls," he said, gesturing at the flowery decorated wallpaper covered walls of her bedroom.

"I promise," Ashley said, hoping she could keep her word. "Was it something worse?"

He stood up and started pacing around her room in deep thought. "Much. When we were in El Paso, I did some more things to get me into trouble."

"Like what?"

He hesitated for a second before answering. "I've got into some trouble for watching girls, and…"

Ashley interrupted, "There's nothing wrong with that. I watch guys all the time when I'm at school or at the mall."

Jake was not smiling. "That's not what I mean by 'watching' girls."

"Well then, what?" she asked cautiously.

"You promise you won't tell anyone no matter how bad this is?" he asked, dead serious.

"I already promised you once that I wouldn't. I haven't changed my mind since then," she repeated her vow.

He regarded her suspiciously for a moment. "I was at the age when I really started noticing the other girls in my classes. The problem was, they didn't seem to notice me. I always sat at the back of the classrooms and kept quiet. I didn't do anything to be noticed. It had a lot to do with the pills that I was on."

Ashley nodded her head, watching him walk from one side of the room to the other. She found it surprising that he did not get *any* attention from other girls.

"I was really lonely in that school. If you weren't a cowboy or a redneck, nobody paid much attention to you. Then, when I figured out that, for as long as I was at that school, that I was probably going to stay lonely, and I started watching some girls I liked."

Without thinking, Ashley asked. "What do you mean? How did you do it?"

Silently, Jake pointed out her window towards a tall maple tree. Ashley followed his finger. It took a moment for it to dawn on her.

"Oh, my God. You watch from the trees?" she asked incredulously.

He just nodded his head, giving it a moment to sink in for Ashley.

"That's one way," he admitted. "I just figured out where some of these girls lived, and if I could figure out a way to, I'd hide outside of their bedroom windows and just watch them."

"Did you watch them just to see if you could see them undress?" Ashley asked, getting scared.

"Not necessarily." He smiled. "If they did that, it was a bonus. No, I enjoyed watching them watch television, talk on the phone, do their homework, or just sleep. I don't know why, it just seemed like that by spying on them when they were in private, it made me feel like I was their friend, that I was a part of their life. My dad caught me sneaking out of the house one night on my way to do this, but I lied and told him I was just going to walk down to the store to get a candy bar. I'm pretty sure that he didn't believe me."

"What makes you say that?"

"It was nearly midnight when he caught me," he said. "A couple days later, my dad saw something in the paper that said that there was a reported peeping tom in our neighborhood. He put two and two together and figured out that I was the culprit. He didn't tell anyone, not even my mom. He confronted me about it, and I couldn't lie to him. He snapped me out of it and made me stop doing it. But to make sure that I wouldn't get caught, we moved to Charlotte over that summer. I didn't do that any in Charlotte, but I have here."

This confession made Ashley shrink back in disgust. "Have you . . ." she started say loudly before Jake could put a hand over her mouth.

"Keep your voice down," he said harshly. "If you want me to keep talking, you've got to be a big girl and keep your voice down. Okay?"

Ashley nodded her head under his hand. He slowly took his hand away from her face. She looked terrified now.

"Have you heard enough? Do you want me to stop?" he asked.

Ashley knew that, as scared as she was of him now, she had to know more. "No," she said.

"Ask your question."

"Have you ever done that to me?" she asked, clutching a hand to her chest.

He was the one who looked scared now, unsure whether he should go answer. "Yes."

Ashley had never felt more violated. All at once, she knew she did not want to hear anymore, and she could not stand to look at him anymore.

"Get out!" she said, looking away, careful not to raise her voice. "Don't ever come back to my house. If you do, I'll call the police. I'll keep your secret. I just want you to leave and never speak to me again."

He stood up slowly from the bed. "I'll leave." He kneeled close to her face. She still couldn't bring herself to look at him. "If you *ever* tell anyone what I said, you'll regret it."

He stood up, walked out of her bedroom, and closed the door without another word, leaving Ashley weeping on her bed. She could not believe this was happening. Her last friend in the world had just threatened her. She had only one person she could turn to.

She thought of something that caused her to pause as she reached for the phone. He did not finish his story. She interrupted him before he could finish. Had he gotten into trouble for something else?

He led off by saying he watched girls through their windows. He was going to say something else. She assumed they caught him watching the girls, and he said that was why they left El

Paso. He said he did not do that in Charlotte, but he did not say why his family left there. Did he do the same thing there or something worse? Not knowing the rest of his story horrified her almost as much as the confession of him watching her through her window.

She left the phone untouched in its cradle. She waited about ten minutes after hearing her front door closed to venture forth from her room.

She needed to talk to her best friend face-to-face.

***

After Jake closed Ashley's bedroom door behind him, he walked down the hallway towards her darkened living room. When he reached the living room, he found it vacant. He looked around the walls of the living room.

As he had observed the first time that he set foot in this house, her dad was obviously a sportsman. He had two deer heads hanging from opposite corners of the room, and on the third wall, the biggest bass that he had ever seen was on display. Not that he had seen many bass in his life. Underneath the bass plaque, Jake could see a picture of Ashley's dad holding up the now showcased fish. In the other corner of the room was her dad's gun cabinet.

He walked over to the doorway, still studying the gun cabinet while putting his shoes on. He did not think her dad put a lock on it. At least he couldn't see one. That showed that Ashley's dad trusts his family. However, Jake was not family.

Loose threads of a grand idea formed in different parts of his mind.

He stood up and looked down the hall towards Ashley's room. The light glowed underneath the door, but he did not figure she would come out anytime soon if she knew what was good for her. Her parents' bedroom was on the opposite end of the house. He looked down at the other hall in that direction. There were no lights on underneath their door.

The threads of thought twisted together to form a plan that would give him his goal. It was so clear.

He quietly padded across the room and knelt by the door to the gun cabinet.

He could do it. He could have *her*.

CHAPTER THIRTY-ONE

In the autumn, people from all around come to see the leaves change color in our area. Something about our little corner of the state led to breathtaking views of fall colors. The leaves change from a lush, vibrant green to all manner of earth tone colors. Brown, yellow, and orange leaves abound. It makes for a beautiful sight.

People celebrate the occasion. Richwood, the other semi-large town in our county, holds a Fall Foliage Festival to celebrate the changing of the leaves. Artisans and women of every sort come to the town that week to hawk their wares. You can buy many homemade crafts. A person can buy everything from homemade jewelry to beautiful autumn themed paintings at what some would consider being bargain prices.

I don't see what all the fuss is about. To me, it seems like from the first moment I see a leaf changing color on a tree, to when the last one falls to the ground takes about a week from beginning to end. People get caught up in it, and I don't know why.

These are the random thoughts that rolled through my head as I prepared for bed and for school the next day. I felt like an automaton going through the same routine, five nights a week: do my homework, watch a little television, talk some with

Elizabeth, brush my teeth, etc., etc. The whole routine was getting old. I wished I were finished with high school. I'm glad that graduation is in sight.

As I prepared to climb into bed, I heard the doorbell ring. I looked over at the alarm clock on my nightstand, which never gets set, and saw it was a little after eleven o'clock.

I heard my dad come from their bedroom, go down the stairs, and open the door. A few moments later, I heard him yell, "Lucas!"

For some reason, I was not surprised it was for me.

I rushed downstairs, wondering who could be at the door at this hour. When I reached the bottom of the stairs, all I could see was my dad with his back turned to me, shielding whoever was at the door.

"Who is it?" I asked, as my dad stepped aside to reveal a teary-eyed Ashley standing in the doorway.

When she looked at me, I knew something horrible had happened. She looked like she had been hurt but showed no physical signs of it. I hurried to Ashley as my dad stood aside. She enveloped me in a big bear hug as soon as I came close enough.

"What's the matter?" I asked.

I caught my dad's eye, giving the signal for privacy. He nodded. He climbed the stairs, and we heard his bedroom door close.

Ashley broke her grip on me.

"Come on," I said, leading her over to the sofa by the front door.

I deposited her weeping form on the sofa, went to the kitchen, and poured her a glass of water. I grabbed a tissue box from a side table on my way back from the kitchen to the sofa. I sat down next to her, handing her both items.

"Thanks," she said, taking a sip of water and then wiping her nose.

It seemed like it had been a long time since I had been this close to her. I knew why she kept her distance, even though I never told Elizabeth what I knew. Now that she was here in my living room, I realized how much I missed being around her.

This was not the time for these thoughts, however. Now was the time for me to worry about my friend. Whatever thoughts or feelings I had on the subject, I pushed it aside. It looked like she was really in a time of need, and I was the one she came to for help at this late hour.

I cleared my head and prepared myself for whatever she was going to tell me.

"Lucas," she said with a nasally voice, "I'm sorry for how I've been acting towards you and Elizabeth. I haven't been very mature."

I didn't argue. "It's been hard on me too, knowing what you were going through, and knowing there was nothing I could do about it."

Somehow, I couldn't imagine this was what brought her over here so late. If this was the reason, it must have really been distressing to her.

"You don't have to apologize," she sniffled. "I was the one who chose not to speak to you and Elizabeth. But that's not the problem."

"What is it?" I encouraged her, suddenly sorry that the big problem was not about our current relationship. I could only think of one thing that would bring her over here this time of night if it had nothing to do with our relationship: something happened between her and Jake.

"Jake threatened me," she blurted out after a few seconds.

I immediately felt an emotion rise in me I do never remember feeling towards another person before: rage. I felt my face and neck flush like they usually do when I get upset.

"What happened?" I asked through clenched teeth.

She caught my reaction, and the drama from these past few weeks washed away in her eyes. I could see that she knew from my reaction that I was here for her and made the correct decision to come to me for help.

"He let on that if I told anyone what he told me, that he would harm me."

"You can tell me. What did he say?"

She seemed to struggle with some sort of inner demon that would not let her talk. She tucked her legs underneath her. I let her think about it, not pressuring her. If she wanted to tell me what it was, he said, she would tell me when she was ready. I thought that tonight, she just needed a friend to be there for her. I could do that if that was what she wanted. I was glad she was speaking to me again, and again I realized how much I missed being around her. I always felt comfortable with her.

I had my arm around her in a protective gesture while she stewed. I let her take her time getting her thoughts together. She took a long drink of water from the glass and pulled out another tissue to blow her nose. She seemed to have made up her mind.

"Okay," she said. "You have got to promise me you will tell no one else about this. If Jake ever finds out I told you this, I don't know what he would do to me."

"I'll protect you," I promised. "I won't let him do anything to you."

"Thanks," she said, giving me a quick hug. She took a deep breath. "He's been lying to everyone, and I think he's up to no good."

"Ok, just start from the beginning. What has Jake been lying about?"

Her statement did not surprise me. Something did not strike me as being right about him from the beginning.

"He has told everyone that he has lived in so many places because his father's company moves him around a lot." I nodded my head. I had heard the story before. "Well, that's only part of the story."

"What's the complete story?"

"Jake has told people that his father's company keeps transferring him. That is only part of the truth. The whole truth, Jake told me, is that his dad *requests* these job transfers to get out of town whenever Jake tarnishes the family name, or something like that."

"What does Jake do to 'tarnish the family name'?"

"Well, I didn't get all the details because I interrupted him after he told me about the first couple of things."

"What did he tell you?" I asked, as she took another sip of water. I saw her glass was nearly empty. I got up, poured her a refill, and returned to her side.

"Thanks," she said as I sat down again. "He said that when they lived in Seattle—"

"I didn't know that he lived there," I interrupted. "I'm sorry, go on."

"He also lived in El Paso and Charlotte too, though I think you knew about Charlotte. Anyway, when he lived in Seattle, he went on some kind of destruction rampage one night and broke a bunch of windows in some of his rich neighbor's homes."

"Really?" That just sounded to me like something a typical rebellious teenager would do. "So, did he get in trouble?"

"No, not really," she continued. "His dad paid all the people off to keep them from pressing charges against Jake. He gave them some extra cash on top of the damages as an extra incentive to keep silent."

I raise my eyebrows at this. "So, that's it? His dad just threw some money around and swept it all under the rug?"

"Yeah," she said, taking another sip of water. "That's what it sounded like. Then his parents took him to a therapist to see what the problem with him was."

"I take it that this wasn't just some isolated incident?"

"No, it wasn't. He told me something else that he had done, but I don't think I need to tell you about it. The only thing that you need to know about that is, is that he was going through a difficult time."

Jake didn't have my sympathy, but it made me wonder what else he did she was leaving out. "Go on," I urged. "Did the therapist figure anything out?"

"Yeah, they ran some tests on him and diagnosed him with bipolar disorder."

I had heard of people being bipolar but wasn't clear on exactly what it was. All I know is that when I hear of bipolar disorder, it is usually in the context of someone that is crazy. I voiced this opinion to her.

"I don't know," she said. "He doesn't really seem crazy to me. He may be a little unbalanced sometimes, but not crazy. I think he is just disturbed. He needs friends, but he doesn't seem to know how to get them, of if he gets one, like me, he doesn't seem to know how to hang on to them for very long."

"Socially inept," I said under my breath.

"What did you say?"

"I said that it sounds like that he is just socially inept. That's what they call people who are like what you describe Jake to be. They can't get friends, and they can't keep the friends that they have either," I explained, recalling a chapter from my Psychology class last year. "Sometimes they tend to withdraw from others after a while. Or sometimes," I hesitated.

"Or sometimes . . ." she prodded.

"Or sometimes they go off the deep end. They do stuff to gain attention. Vandalism is one of the main ways for them to get attention. In extreme cases, they even try to commit suicide to get attention."

When I said that, she gasped. I did not ask why she gasped, but I now suspect that this was what she was holding back.

I tried to make her feel better. "They never really intend to commit suicide, and it's just an attention-getting device."

"That is what it sounds like he was doing," she agreed, divulging at least one secret she was harboring.

"They said that he had bipolar . . .," I said reminding her of where she left off in her story.

"Yeah. They put him on some meds and a while later, they up and moved to El Paso."

"Wow, that's a big move."

"That's what I said too."

"Did he go back to normal when they moved to El Paso?"

"No, they had him on so many pills that he said he wasn't the same. The people there differed from what he was used to, and he couldn't make any friends there, so he got extremely lonely."

I knew that even if he was on medications or not, sometimes if one gets desperate enough, medications are not enough to keep a person under control. Sometimes the disorder would rear its ugly head from time to time.

Knowing this, I asked, "What did he do?"

She sighed. "He told me they had to move because his dad figured out he's some sort of peeping tom. He said he liked to sit up in trees outside of girl's windows and watch girls undress and do whatever. And rather than wait for someone else to figure out that it was Jake, his dad decided to move to Charlotte."

I knew that what she had to say would be bad. I just figured that maybe he broke some more windows or something. However, this was on a whole weirder level. I thought his dad must have some incredibly deep pockets to afford to move around that much.

"That's horrible," I said. What she said sickened me.

She had a look on her face that told me she felt dirty just for saying it.

I thought about the tree outside of Ashley's window and wondered if he had done that to Ashley. I recalled the layout of Elizabeth's home. She had no tree outside of her window, thank goodness, but I believed there was one outside of her bathroom. This was a horrifying thought, that maybe this psycho had been violating two of my best friends without them knowing about it.

"Then I threw him out, when he said that he had watched me before," she said, almost apologetically.

"Well good! What did he do then?"

"That's when he threatened me," she revealed. "He did that and then left without another word. I waited for about ten minutes after he left before I came over here. Lucas, you're the only one that I know I could turn to," she said, placing a burden on my shoulders. "If I told my dad, he would have killed him."

"Yeah, he would have," I said, imagining Jake's head among all those animal trophies on her living room wall. I don't think her day would respond well to threats. She at least giggled at what I said. "Well, Ashley, what do you want for *me* to do?"

"First, can we go back to the way we were? I miss you so much. And Elizabeth too, of course," she said quickly, realizing that she had inadvertently left Elizabeth out. "I have been so lonely since our falling out. I had to have someone to talk to, and Jake was the only one who would."

That, at least, explained how she and Jake got together.

"Do you think we can go back to how we were before?" she asked. "I mean, I don't want to come between you and Elizabeth, but I miss the three of us."

"Of course, we can," I answered without hesitation. "It has been hard on me too, not having my main girl to talk to," I said and meant it, knowing that my main girl was supposed to be Elizabeth. Ashley was my main girl of a different sort.

She practically glowed when I told her this, as if all her worries were over.

"What about Jake? We can't let him go around doing what he told me he has been doing."

"I don't know if we can do anything," I said. "If he knows he's being watched, or that he has been alerted to the cop's attention, he will know that you've told someone about what he said. I think for now, we do nothing, we'll just go to school tomorrow as though nothing happened, and hopefully we can catch him in the act or something, and he'll just go away again."

"But that's not all," she reminded me.

"Oh, that's right. You said you interrupted him before he could finish."

"Yeah, he told me about the watching the girls from the trees, and he was getting ready to confess something else when I cut him off."

"If he led off with watching girls, the second thing could have been worse."

"That's exactly what I thought after he left. Or it may not have been. But that's what scares me. How could we find out? I'm not going to talk to him again. And if I did, and that's what I ask him about, he would get suspicious."

"I agree." My mind was running at a hundred miles an hour now, trying to come up with solutions. "The only thing that I can think that we can try without him finding out that we are looking into him would be to get on to the internet and see if there is a trail that we can follow. I would bet that the reason that they left Charlotte was over something that he had done or was doing. That would fit the frequent move pattern."

"I hope we can find something. What are you going to tell Elizabeth?"

I thought about her question for a second before answering. I don't want to tell Ashley about not telling Elizabeth that I knew why Ashley had not been speaking to us. I never told her about what Ashley revealed to me in that locker room. I realized that this might be the way to approach this situation as well.

"Nothing. I don't want her to know anything about this. You know, if she found out, it would be all over the school two seconds after we tell her, and we can't let that happen. I think that in this situation, for her, ignorance would be bliss."

"I was hoping we could keep this between us," she said, wrapping me in an embrace. "Lucas, I'm so glad that you're my friend."

"Ashley, I can't imagine having a better friend," I told her, kissing her on top of the head. "It's getting late, and I think we should call it a night. We both need to get some sleep. You do especially."

"Yeah," she said, standing up. "Can you give me a ride home?"

I looked out the window and saw that her car wasn't out there. "Did you walk over here?"

"No, I didn't trust myself to drive. Besides, it wasn't that cold outside when I started out. It's gotten colder since I left the house," she smiled.

I slipped my shoes on, and called up to mom and dad, and told them where I was going. They understood and told me to be careful at this late hour.

Before we walked out the door, Ashley gave me an even bigger hug than before. "Thank you so much," she whispered. I could feel the warmth of her breath in my ear.

"Ashley, anytime, that you need anything, just know that I'm always here for you no matter what," I whispered.

"I know," she said, releasing the hug. "That's why I came to you."

On the ride over to her house, she said to me, "He talks about you, you know?"

"He talks about me? That's creepy."

"No," she laughed. "I get the impression that he looks up to you or something."

"Why would he look up to me? He could have fooled me. He doesn't seem to like me too well."

"No, let me rephrase that: I think he wishes he was like you."

"What about me? I'm just a normal guy. I play sports, and luckily have a girlfriend," I pointed out, although that may have touched a sour note by mentioning Elizabeth.

"Because of him, his family hasn't lived in the same area for more than a year or two at a time," she explained. "That's just it. He never played many school sports. They usually have to move before he can establish any long-lasting friends. He has never had what we consider having a normal life, and I think he sees in you what he would like to strive for if he were normal."

"I think Coach Wheeler mentioned Jake started on the football team when he lived in North Carolina. So, he has played team sports before."

"Yeah, but he only lived there for part of this year. Do you think you could make any real friends in that short of time?"

I thought about it for a second, and then answered, "You're right. I don't think that *I* could. Maybe a few acquaintances, but I don't know about being able to establish a tight relationship in a short amount of time. Has he ever had any girlfriends?"

"None that he mentioned. It would suit that if he was lonely enough to stalk girls, he wasn't exactly swimming in them," she answered. "But as far as I know, he's never really had an actual girlfriend."

"Wow. I couldn't imagine that kind of life. But that doesn't give him an excuse to do to you what he did."

"Yeah, well, unfortunately for him, I'm not going to be talking to him anymore after what he pulled tonight."

The temperature dropped once the sun went down. The moon shone in a starlit sky. I dropped her off at her front door, where she gave me a kiss on the cheek and thanked me again before she exited the car.

As I drove home, I thought about what she told me about Jake. I had thought that there was something suspicious about him, but I did not know what. Now that I know I had a reason to be suspicious, I wished I didn't know.

Now that Ashley had piqued my interest, I wanted to know more. I wanted to know why they left Charlotte. Ashley was right. He broke the ice by telling her about vandalism, peeping toms, and, I assumed, a suicide attempt.

What could have been so horrible that he was saving it for last?

CHAPTER THIRTY-TWO

Jake was enjoying the freedom of living without medication. He could talk to people more. He felt more normal. He had times such as now where he felt unbelievably happy. That is weird, because only twenty minutes ago, he was angry to the point of threatening the person who used to be his best friend. He realized that was weird, but was so overjoyed now, he didn't care.

While strolling down the road towards his home, he took a minor detour. There was no hurry. His parents knew he might be out late. This time, he had an excuse for not coming home until late. All that he needed to say if anyone asked him was that he was over at Ashley's until late studying for an English exam.

The sky was clear. The stars glowed in the night sky. When you live in a city or a large town, there are so many lights that they block out the stars. This was the first place he had lived in his life where he could go out and see the stars. He thought they were a beautiful and magnificent thing of beauty.

Of course, he had lived here for two months before he ever noticed them, thanks to the medications. Not only did his meds keep him from having sudden mood swings, they also kept him from being able to enjoy some of the common things in life.

When he was on his pills, his mom could make him his favorite lasagna, and he could eat half of it, knowing it tasted good, but not really seem to care. He could watch a movie that he heard was excellent and would fit in with other movies he liked, and it would seem bland to him.

He felt like one of the zombies he regularly blasted in his video games.

When they moved up here into the mountains, he could not appreciate the beauty of the tree-covered gently rolling mountains of sandstone and limestone. He had seen the Rocky Mountains before with their jagged edges and snow-covered peaks. They were much higher in elevation than the Appalachian Mountains that he now lived in. Those were majestic. But these ancient densely forested mountains of West Virginia would always appeal to him.

He rarely noticed these things while on his pills. Now that he had been off them for a couple of weeks, he was seeing what all life offered again. He was also noticing that he could feel happy again. That was a feeling that he missed. He did not welcome back, however, the lows of his newfound freedom.

He would have times when he would sit on his bed up in his room with his knees held to his chest, wishing that he had never been born. Deep down, he knew he had no reason to feel the way he did. He knew he had parents who loved him and tried whatever they could to protect him, even if that meant they had to make sacrifices in their personal lives just to do that. When they settled into a new town, his dad would make some new friends at work, and his mom would likewise make some friends from around whatever neighborhood they lived in.

Jake, however, could never seem to make any friends and he would get lonely. Then, because of his loneliness, he would do something bad, and he had to admit that he was just trying to get some attention from someone when he did these things. Then his parents would choose to sacrifice whatever connections they had made in their personal lives to provide Jake with the opportunity to make friends somewhere else. Then they were on the move again.

Jake had been unsuccessful in making friends yet here in Mt. Lookout or at school in Summersville, but he was making inroads since going off of his pills. He found that by contributing more in class, the other kids seemed to notice he wasn't the monster everyone seemed to think he was when he first started school here. He was trying to talk to more people, and he was seeing those efforts pay off.

However, the one person he still could not get to talk to him was Elizabeth. He had lived in Seattle, seen all the pretty mid-western girls living in El Paso, had seen some beauties that were talked about all over North Carolina. None of them were as beautiful in his eyes as Elizabeth. Elizabeth's boyfriend, Jake assumed, was the reason she would not talk to him.

He was looking at her now. She did not know it, though. He was watching her from the oak tree situated outside of her window. She was brushing her teeth. She had on a pair of gray sweatpants and a white NCHS t-shirt with one hand on the sink, balancing her as she leaned forward to get a better look in the mirror. God, she looked so good.

Jake was extremely cold sitting up high in the tree on a thick limb. He figured the temperature had to be near freezing, and all he wore was a light jacket. When he went over to Ashley's, he had expected her to drive him home after their 'study' session was over. He could not have known that he would screw up and have to walk home.

He really had little interest in Ashley to begin with. He had hoped that getting near Ashley would provide the doorway to getting near Elizabeth. It was just his bad luck that he picked a time to make a move on Ashley when the two girls weren't getting along very well.

He stuck it out with Ashley hoping she and Elizabeth would make up and be friends again. Before they could do that, he had to go and possibly mess everything up by confessing to Ashley about his past. He felt like he needed to tell someone the truth. He did not know she would respond the way she did, but he hoped for her sake, she didn't tell anyone. If word got out about what he told her, he could almost guarantee himself that no one would give him a second look, and that would prove bad for Ashley. That was what happened in Charlotte before things went south there.

Elizabeth was washing off some kind of facial mask she had put on before brushing her teeth. He knew from the other couple of times that he had sat on this branch at night that this was the end of her nightly routine. Usually, doing this was exhilarating for him. Tonight, however, with the events that happened earlier in the evening, he could not seem to get any satisfaction out of watching her. It was just something to do.

The moment of heightened joy must be over, he thought.

He watched her dry her hands and face on a hand towel, turn out the light, and walk out of the bathroom. The show was over. Jake climbed down from the tree as quietly as he could, taking care not to damage the package that he now had in his jacket pocket.

He stayed low to the ground as he made his way back to the side of the road. There was very little traffic at this time of night in Mt. Lookout.

Now that he had ruined whatever he had going with Ashley, he had to scrap that part of the plan. He would not be getting to Elizabeth through Ashley now. Therefore, he would have to convince Lucas to break up with her. Lucas was so enamored of her that Jake strongly doubted that he could talk Lucas into breaking up with Elizabeth.

That was what he was hoping his new little friend in his pocket would help him do. In Jake's mind, there did not seem to be any flaws in this plan. He saw while Plan B may be extreme, there was no way it could fail.

CHAPTER THIRTY-THREE

Clouds rolled in after midnight, pregnant with moisture. That and the falling temperatures brought a dusting of snow. The thin, white layer of snow was not enough to call for a delay, but it made the drive to school more of a challenge than usual. We left for school ten minutes sooner than we usually would, so we could take our time.

We did not run into any problems, and I made it to home-room a good five minutes before the bell sounded. Mrs. Gibson had a surprised look on her face when she saw Allen and I walk in. I thought she was going to say something to us about being early, but she smiled and went back to planning her lessons for the day. I took that as a compliment coming from her.

It looked as if Ashley and Elizabeth had made up, as they were talking animatedly about something, laughing the whole time. I walked over and said good morning to both. Elizabeth stood up and gave me a hug.

"Ashley apologized to me," she whispered in my ear. "I told her that there was nothing to apologize for."

"Good," I said. She released the hug and sat back down. I turned to Ashley. "How are you?"

"Much better this morning," she said, smiling up at me. I saw her look behind me, and her expression darkened. I knew what that meant.

Jake must have arrived.

We continued talking as Jake slid past me on the way to his seat. He said 'good morning' to all of us. Elizabeth and I returned it. Ashley sat silent. Elizabeth was now facing forward in her chair with her back to Ashley. Behind Elizabeth, Ashley shook her head at me and held a finger to her lips. I nodded as the bell sounded and went to my seat.

***

Ashley stuck close to me during gym class helping me with my assistant duties, which consisted of setting up and taking down the Ping-pong tables, getting out whatever equipment Coach Nixon needed from the storage closet, and generally staying out of the way of the rest of the class. She told him she wasn't feeling well and asked to be excused from going through the daily exercises.

We tried hard to avoid being near Jake, while it looked like Jake was trying to stay away from us.

At one point, Ashley said to me, "What am I going to do next period?"

She told me she sat in front of Jake during their English class. I was afraid something might happen.

"Just try to avoid him, if possible," I advised.

"Yeah, like that'll be easy," she said. "I mean, what if he says something to me? Just because I told him not to speak to me, it doesn't mean he's going to respect my wishes."

"I don't know what to tell you. All I can tell you is that you can handle it. I know you. You're one tough hombre," I kidded, giving her a playful punch in the shoulder.

"Whatever," she smiled, rubbing her shoulder even though I know I did not hit her near hard enough for it to hurt. "Lucas, you always know how to make me feel better."

"Thanks," I said. That felt awkward.

"You know what?" she asked after a few seconds.

"What?"

"I can handle it," she said with resolve.

Coach Nixon told everyone to go change as the class was ending. Ashley thanked me and headed off toward the locker room.

I just hoped Jake behaved himself next period.

CHAPTER THIRTY-FOUR

The truth was that Ashley was not as tough or in control of her emotions as she portrayed herself to be. On the outside, she acted as though nothing had happened the previous night. On the inside, she was a total mess. She wrestled with the temptation of staying home from school so she would not have to see Jake. She had to come to school. Everyone that knew her knew that if Ashley was absent from school, then something had to be seriously wrong. In her life, there had only been two days when she missed school.

Once in Elementary School, she had chicken pox, and had to miss a week of school. The other time she missed a day was to attend her grandmother's funeral. Had she not been at school today, classmates and teachers would have noticed, and somebody would have said something about her not being there. Jake had not been around long enough to know about her exemplary attendance. Ashley knew Jake would know *why* she was not there. She wanted him to think his threat did not bother her.

As she walked from the gym to her locker to pick up her English book, she could feel Jake following somewhere behind her. It made her sick to think about what he had done to her.

She wondered if he was watching her right now in the way he had before. She felt violated just being near him.

She risked a quick glance behind her and confirmed her fear. Jake was about seven feet behind her, staring at a hole in the back of her head, though there were several students between the two of them. He wore his black overcoat on again, hands jammed in the pockets. Ashley had not seen him wearing that jacket since he first started school here. No one has worn those types of trench coats in this school ever since the Columbine incident out in Colorado. Of course, he could wear it until some teacher told him to remove it.

She reached her locker and grabbed her English book as quickly as she could. Jake struggled to get his locker open several lockers away. He had his back to Ashley, so at least he was not trying to make eye contact. As she shut her locker door, she rushed off as Jake popped his locker open. At least this way, she could put some distance between the two of them on her way down the hall to the English classroom. It was a small victory, she had to admit, but it made her feel good.

She was uneasy through English class with Jake behind her. She had butterflies in her stomach. He had said nothing to her, and she was thankful for that. The teacher, Mrs. Davis, went through her lesson and gave them an assignment out of their textbook. She then took her seat behind a cluttered desk at the front of the room.

Ashley was deep in concentration, trying hard to concentrate on breaking down complex sentences, when she felt a forceful grip on her shoulder. Jake.

"I saw you talking to Lucas," he whispered harshly in her ear. "Did you tell him anything?" Ashley shook her head. "Good. If I hear rumors about you know what, I'll know where they came from, and you will regret it." She nodded her head again, this time the other way. "Good."

He removed his hand, and that was the end of it. Ashley thought she was going to pee her pants or cry. She was very frightened now.

***

Lunch made things better for Ashley. She took up a spot at the table where she used to sit beside Elizabeth. Lucas had come by and apologized to them. He had to go to the library to work on a report and could not eat with them. Ashley was disappointed, as was Elizabeth, but that gave the two of them some time to catch up on things.

"How are you and Lucas doing?" Ashley asked, taking a bite of Salisbury steak.

"Okay, I guess," Elizabeth said, munching on a salad. "At the beginning, it was wonderful. You know the newness of it, getting to know each other differently. It was exciting. But now, we've gotten into a routine."

Elizabeth's bluntness surprised Ashley. She didn't expect that answer. Not all was perfect in Dreamland between Lucas and Elizabeth.

"Oh, okay," Ashley said, not really knowing what to say.

"But I haven't had a better boyfriend," Elizabeth stated.

"And you've had a lot of them," Ashley finished for her, nearly making Elizabeth spit out the milk she was drinking.

She set her milk down, laughing. She laid her hand on Ashley's arm. "Oh Ashley, I missed you."

"I've missed you too."

CHAPTER THIRTY-FIVE

During the lunch hour, the school provided several avenues the students could use to keep themselves occupied. They do this because the Commons Area was not big enough to accommodate all six hundred students at the same time. I believed there was probably a fire code against that. Of course, they encouraged all students to have lunch in the Commons Area, and most do. Students are also allowed to sit in the hallways running beside the auditorium and the gymnasium to eat if they so wish. They also open the gym so that some can play basketball. Because our school schedule only allows for four classes in a day, about half of the kids in school at any given semester do not have a gym class. Therefore, they open the gym during lunchtime to encourage those that do not have gym to get a little exercise.

The other thing students can do is go to the library to do research on the internet. I was going to the library, not to do research for a project, but to do some research on Jake. I promised Ashley that she could help me, but I did not know what I might find. If I found anything, it might be something she could find disturbing. It could be something I found disturbing, but I was prepared. I just did not want to have Ashley go through any more emotional distress about this than she already has.

I had my biology book under my arm, so the librarian would think I was doing research on something in my textbook. I hoped she would not ask what I was studying. I liked to keep my bases covered.

There were six computer partitions in one corner of our small library. They fit into a rectangle with three computers making up each side of the rectangle. At present, four of the computers are in use. I walked over to the librarian and requested one of the open computers. She looked down at my book, smiled, and told me to take computer station number three. The number three station was on one end of the computer partitions. A slightly overweight girl with a pink sweater occupied the station next to it.

As I sat down, I noticed her screen displayed a dieting website. As I settled into my chair, I smiled at her. She smiled back. A cute smile. I didn't know what her name was, but if she had any success in her diet, she could be a knockout.

I opened the web browser and went directly to Google. I thought of a subject I might encounter in my biology class and typed in a search for humpback whales. I clicked on the first link that I saw, simply labeled 'Humpback Whales.' A page popped open, showing the scientific name and a diagram for a humpback.

This should suffice.

I knew the girl next to me was not looking at anything I would consider being a class subject. That told me the librarian wasn't paying much attention to the websites the other three students were looking at. Still, it was smart to play it safe, just in case.

Satisfied that the librarian wasn't looking, I minimized the whales and opened another tab. That way, if the librarian came over to see what I was looking at, I could just click on the whales in the other tab, and she would see that I was studying up on humpbacks. It wouldn't hold up under scrutiny, but considering what the girl next to me was looking at, I felt a close examination probably wasn't forthcoming.

I knew what Jake wanted was attention. I would not put it past him to make something up just to get a little sympathy from Ashley. I was going to see if I could corroborate his story.

I hoped I could find all I needed to know on the internet. I someone's name shows up in a police or newspaper report, you can find what you need to know. I hoped I would find nothing, and just go on believing that Jake was just another troubled classmate.

With this new browser up, I typed '**Jake Schofield**' on the search bar. I clicked the search button, and I saw Google found nearly two hundred thousand links containing the words '**Jake Schofield**.' That was not going to work. On the search bar, I re-entered "**Jake Schofield**", but this time I put quotation marks around his name.

I learned in my internet class last year that if you search on Google and put quotation marks around what you are looking for, it would find only those sites that contain those words just as you typed them. The first time that I tried, Google just found every occurrence where it found either '**Jake**' or '**Schofield**' on any page.

I clicked the search button again. This narrowed it down to a more manageable two hundred links. There were links to a street hockey website, an Executive Philanthropy Board, and a motocross leader board, to name a few. Jake did not seem like the street hockey type, surely not a philanthropist or a motocross racer. I scrolled down the first few pages of links and saw nothing of interest.

Ashley had told me that Jake had told her he had gotten into some trouble watching girls through their windows. If he had gotten into any real trouble, something like that would have ended up in a report somewhere. If he were under sixteen years of age, a published report would not have printed his name. They could only refer to him as a 'minor'. In some states, I thought you had to be over eighteen before they publish your name in the newspaper. I figured Jake was under sixteen when he lived in El Paso. I doubted that trying to use his name to find out information from when he lived in El Paso wasn't going to work.

I kept thinking about it. I forget sometimes that Google is also one of the biggest news websites as well. I clicked on the news link. Maybe this would help provide better results.

I went back to the search bar, and this time typed in 'El Paso peeping Tom'. I thought 'peeping Tom' was what they referred to someone such as Jake in the media. This time, I saw only one link.

My pulse quickened. I clicked on the link.

<u>Crime Tracker Alert</u>

From the El Paso Times

04/02/20xx

During the month of March, there were eight reports of a 'Peeping Tom' in the Shady Sands subdivision. In all

eight incidents, when the police arrived to investigate, the "Peeping Tom' subject had vanished. The police currently have no plans for further investigation.

I figured that the 'peeping tom' this article referred to was Jake. The date in the article fit nicely with when I thought Jake lived in El Paso. So, in my mind, I'm inclined to believe what he told Ashley about watching girls was probably true. Why tell the truth about one horrible thing and then make up something else that was not true to go along with it? I thought that what he told her about breaking all those windows probably happened. She also said that he was going to tell her about something else before she ended up kicking him out. But what?

Then the thought struck me. They just moved up here from Charlotte. I'm sure he was at least sixteen when he lived there, and if he was not, I hoped North Carolina was one of those states where they print minor's names. I went back to the search bar and retyped **"Jake Schofield"** in quotation marks. Outside that, I typed '**Charlotte**' and then clicked search.

One link appeared.

As I stared in horror at the headline, I sat back in my seat and made sure no one was watching me. The librarian was down one aisle putting books back on the shelves. The girl beside me was engrossed with whatever diet she was looking at.

My pulse quickened. I felt my cheeks flush. With no one watching, I clicked on the link. The internet connection seemed to go interminably slow. The page took what seemed like forever to load.

When it did. My world changed.

Student Arrested for Pulling a Gun at Independence
08/11/20xx

A bizarre and shocking incident occurred at Independence High School. Yesterday, a student, Jake Schofield, was suspended indefinitely for firing a gun in a crowded hallway between classes. Fortunately, another student saw the assailant pull the gun from his book bag and deflected the gun upward while the assailant was raising his gun from the bag to shoot, causing the errant shot to shoot upwards, destroying a ceiling tile.

Fortunately, no students were harmed in the incident, and it is unclear if the shooter had an intended target. Mr. Schofield is currently being held in police custody for illegal possession of a firearm, firing a weapon in a public place, attempted manslaughter, and attempted murder.

Principal McMahan tells us that Mr. Schofield enrolled at Independence just over three months before this incident occurred, and that he had just moved here from El Paso, Texas. He also said that Mr. Schofield, before this incident, seemed to be a well-behaved student. Jake Schofield starts at safety on the varsity football team.

It was a brief article—one hundred and seventy-five words— but it had a profound effect on me. I remembered hearing about this on the news. I remembered it was a news item for about two days, and then never heard about it again.

I wondered how Jake's dad got him out of this. This was much, much worse than peeking into a girl's windows. Was this what he was going to tell Ashley when he cut her off last night?

The thought made me shiver.

This article was dated nearly ten months after the El Paso article, while not confirmation that the El Paso article was about Jake, was all I needed to know.

I tried to put together a timeline in my head.

During the past couple of years, Jake crashed windows in Seattle, and they moved to El Paso. Then, in the early spring of the following year, this 'peeping tom' mess came about. I assumed Jake's dad somehow made him stop. Then, before he could get into trouble, they moved again. He enrolled in school in Charlotte at the beginning of this school year, and soon after that, he attempted to shoot someone at the school. It took about two months for them to build that house that his family lives in now. He came here sometime towards the end of November. The sequence of events all fit together into a nice, neat timeline.

In my mind, I was convinced that Jake was the 'peeping Tom' mentioned in the article. I also saw in black and white on the glowing computer monitor that he might have also tried to kill someone. Recently. In addition, it may not have been 'someone'; it could have potentially been many 'someone's. The question now was, what do I do with this information?

Before, I thought maybe he was just a pervert. Now, he might be a pervert *and* homicidal. A scary combination.

I needed to see Jake about this before he hurt any of my friends.

I wasn't prepared for what happened next.

CHAPTER THIRTY-SIX

I left the library and rushed towards the Commons Area. I had about fifteen minutes left during lunch. By the time I found Jake, I figured I would have about ten minutes left to confront him.

I hurried through the mostly empty hallways, thinking about what exactly I was going to say to him. I could tell him I knew why he moved up here. Once I told him I could take a few different routes. I could tell him I would keep my mouth closed and not tell anyone if he would leave Ashley, Elizabeth, and me alone. I could say I was going to tell everyone as a way of getting back at him for what he did to Ashley. No one knows why he was here, and I could just imagine everyone's reaction if it came out. I could threaten him in return. I have never threatened bodily harm to anyone, nor have I ever been in a fight. However, I would if it meant keeping my closest friends safe.

I rushed into the Commons Area and looked around. Every table was crowded, but I could not think of a time that I have seen Jake eating in here recently. I saw Ashley and Elizabeth sitting across from each other at their usual table, with Ashley facing towards me. We made eye contact. I waved and rushed towards the gym, leaving her with a confused look on her face.

I stood at the entrance of the gym and looked to see if Jake was somewhere in there. The students were clearing out, hoping to get a quick bite to eat before class resumed. I did not see Jake in the thinning crowd.

As I left the gym, the side doors providing access to the student parking lot were to my right. I looked outside and saw dense snow falling through the air. There were a few girls standing there looking out from the floor to ceiling windows at the falling snow. I did not know their names, but I walked up to them and asked if any of them had seen that Jake guy.

One girl with curly, red hair pulled back into a ponytail and large glasses pointed towards the back of the parking lot. "I think I saw him heading off in that direction," she said.

"Thanks," I told her as I pushed open the door.

All I had on was a short-sleeved polo shirt and a pair of Levi's. My jacket was in my locker. The cold enveloped me as soon as I walked out, causing goosebumps to rise on my exposed skin. The girl had pointed off toward where my car was. I jogged off in that direction, looking for him.

I looked down every aisle I passed. Jake was nowhere in sight. I reached my car and saw Jake huddled on the ground by my driver's side door, covered in a thin layer of snow. Surprised, I took a step backwards.

"Hey Jake, what are you doing out here?" I asked, while trying to be friendly. I had to rub my hands on my arms to get some warmth back into them.

"I could ask you the same thing," he said, venom dripping from his voice.

I lied. "I forgot a book in my car."

"It's not in there. I checked."

"What were you doing looking in my car?" I asked, while still trying to be polite.

"I don't know. I just got bored waiting for you."

"Why were you waiting for me?"

"I needed to talk to you. I couldn't find you inside, so I waited out here by your car."

"Yeah, but that wouldn't be for a few hours. You'd freeze to death."

"I can handle the cold," he said. "Do you have your keys on you?"

"Yeah," I said, taking them out of my pocket. "Right here."

"Lay them down on the ground, now."

"I don't think so, Jake."

He stood up, pulled a gun out of his pocket, and pointed it in my general direction.

My eyes widened. My heart thumped in my chest.

He repeated, "I said, lay them down on and kick them over here. Do anything dumb, like kicking them hard or kicking them away. That will get you killed."

He sounded like he meant it. This time I complied, dropped my keys, and kicked them to him just as he demanded. I was scared to death, but I thought I could get this under control. "Okay, Jake. Take it easy."

He stood and picked up the keys. He kept the gun pointed at me, but low enough that anyone watching from the school wouldn't see that he had a gun in hand over the cars.

"No, I will not 'take it easy.' You have something I want, and now I think we should have a frank discussion about how you are going to give it to me. Get in the car," he said, picking up the keys and gesturing at the passenger door with the gun.

Like a robot, I walked to the door, opened it, and climbed inside. Not once did I consider making a break for it. I buckled my seatbelt as Jake got in on the driver's side and shut the door. He started the car and turned on the windshield wipers to clear away the inch of snow that had already accumulated. He backed out of the spot, and we left the parking lot.

The snow began falling at a heavier rate. It was the thick, wet variety of snow. It was accumulating quickly, making the roads treacherous. I didn't know how well Jake knew how to drive, but I will bet that he did not drive in these conditions very often while living in El Paso and Charlotte.

I was sitting next to a guy with a gun aimed directly at my head. I had never been more scared in my life. He had his right hand on the wheel, with the gun in his left hand pointed at me. I couldn't imagine where he got the gun. I knew he had one in Charlotte. I couldn't imagine this being the same one. I'm sure that at some point it was confiscated. Then again, most everyone in West Virginia has a gun hiding somewhere in their house, car, or self. However, the only person I knew Jake had been around who owns guns was Ashley's dad. Maybe Jake stole it from his gun cabinet at some point.

As we sped down Route 19, I prayed to myself that there would be a couple of cop cars along the way to wherever Jake was taking me. He was going well over the speed limit and having a hard time keeping the car in one lane. The police in this town itch to pull people so they can write them a large speeding ticket. They would also write the driver another one for reckless driving, passing over the centerline, or whatever charge they made up.

For once, I didn't see any cops. Perhaps they figured if people were going to drive the way Jake was driving in this snowstorm that they would just let them kill themselves. The one time they sat at the station, eat donuts, and sip coffee, of course, would be the one time I needed them.

"Do you know why I hate you?" he asked.

"I didn't know that you 'hated' me." I tried to shift as far against the window as I could to put what little distance I could between that gun and me. "I thought maybe you had a problem with me or something, but I didn't know why."

"Because you have the life I want, the girl I want, and I know I can't have them!"

His outburst reverberated through the enclosed space of the car. I've never known anyone to be jealous of me for anything. I tried to think quickly about what to do, how to get out of this. I needed an escape plan. My mind kept drawing blanks. All I could think of was trying to talk him out of firing that gun.

His tantrum continued. "You've got the cheerleader! You've got a car!"

He stopped shouting for a second and reached up with his gun hand to wipe off some spittle. Even knowing about his bipolar disorder, the sudden mood swing from him being in control of himself to this explosion was still a shock.

I needed to talk to him on an even keel. To reason with him. "But why can't you have all of that?"

"Because they told me I'm nuts! A psychiatrist told my parents I was bi-polar. Whatever that means. After that, they put me on these pills that stripped my personality away. I was boring. I couldn't laugh. I couldn't smile. My friends stopped talking to me. I've got it bad enough that sometimes, not even the pills were enough to keep me controlled. Sometimes something would happen that would cause me to snap anyway, and occasionally, I would go a few days without taking them, just so that I could feel normal again. But as always, my parents would catch on, and force me to take them again."

He stopped speaking for a few seconds as he pulled off Route 19 onto Starbuck St. It was a small street leading to downtown Summersville. This made me feel a little safer pulling off the main highway and onto a street with a much lower speed limit. However, Jake ignored the speed limit. He was going about the same speed down this side street as he did on the main highway.

The difference was that these side streets weren't as clear. They hadn't been treated or plowed, and there hadn't been enough traffic to create drivable ruts in the road. There were less defined ruts for cars to travel in, making for more dangerous travel.

"I take it you're not taking them now," I said, speaking of the medications.

"Good call, genius," he said. "I just wanted to feel normal again."

Now I thought I understood. He wanted a life like mine because he had never had the life that he wanted.

I kept my voice calm. "I know about you pulling that gun out in Charlotte."

His eyes went wide, as it was his turn to look at me in shock. He focused back on the road, shaking his head. "I knew it would eventually get out."

"I haven't told anyone. I just found out about looking it up on the net in the library. I was looking for you just now because I wanted to ask you about it." I tried to make him feel like I was doing him a favor by coming to him first.

"It's good that you didn't with people around. I might have killed you where you stood."

That scared me more, but at least it gave me a glimmer of hope. Like maybe he was going to let me out of this. I don't know what I could do for him other than let him vent his frustrations. Maybe that was all that he needed.

"I also know about you watching those girls in El Paso."

That was a mistake. So much for trying to create an atmosphere of camaraderie. He went ballistic.

"How the hell did you find out about that?"

Now I did not feel as hopeful.

"The same way that I found out about you pulling the gun." I told him how I connected the dots together. "What happened there? In Charlotte?"

Jake took a deep breath and focused on his driving while he collected his thoughts. I could have taken this opportunity to make a grab for the gun while his mind was elsewhere, but I decided I would like to live a little longer. I wasn't ready to die.

"The same thing that happened here, with you finding out about my past, happened there, but on a much larger scale. Some kid found out about what I had done in El Paso and in Seattle and told everyone that he knew in the school about it. He put it on Facebook, Twitter, anywhere kids could read about it. Any hopes that I had of having a good social life were ruined.

"I got so mad at the kid that I had to have revenge for ruining my life. I figured I had to ruin his too," he explained. "I didn't want to kill him, just scare the crap out of him. I've seen that article too. I know it said that I fired the gun, but I had no intention of doing that. It's just when the other stupid kid hit the gun when I was pulling it out and it just went off."

To me, that sounded like an extreme way to make a point, but I did not voice this opinion to him, though. I guessed he was using the same intimidation tactic with me to get my girlfriend. I couldn't very well do that. Even if I broke up with Elizabeth, it was not as though she would go running into his arms. I had the impression from her she found him creepy. As far as I know, girls rarely date guys they find creepy.

"Ashley told you about me watching her?" he said, breaking my train of thought. He knew the answer to his question. He muttered something under his breath that I did not quite catch. I assumed it was probably something derogatory about Ashley.

We were approaching downtown, and we approached the stoplight where Main Street intersected with Starbuck. Jake went left, skidding around the turn, towards downtown, while driving well over the speed limit. The snow was really falling now. Visibility was almost at zero. There were very few cars on the road. That was great because it lessened our probability of hitting one and injuring someone else.

"Jake, have you ever thought about thinking about what you have instead of focusing on what you don't have?" This made him even angrier. I pressed on. "I mean, a person can't have everything they want. Sometimes they have to make do with what they have and create a way to attain what they desire."

My philosophy was lost on him. I knew I was walking an already thin line, and now I had pushed him over the edge.

I knew I was about to die.

He stared, shouting with his eyes locked on me, not on the road. With the snow swirling around us, my car barely maintaining control, my pulse pounding in my eardrums, all I heard was him shouting, "Me! Me! Me!"

I know there were words in between the litany of "me's", but I couldn't focus on them. Instead, my focus was on the gun that he was now tapping up against his chest every time he yelled, "Me!"

"Nobody has ever loved me!"

Tap.

"Nobody has ever cared about me!"

Tap.

"Nobody has ever cared if I do anything with my life!"

Tap.

"All I wanted was to be someone like you!" he yelled, this time extending the gun to point at me to emphasize his last statement.

The gun was so close I could grab it, but I was afraid to. I could smell the oil and cold steel.

"I wanted to be popular with the girls! I just want people to like me!" This time, he resumed tapping his chest with the gun.

I knew now that it was not just about Elizabeth. He just needed a friend and support.

I glanced out the windshield to see that we were rapidly approaching the intersection of Main Street and Broad Street. The busiest intersection in town.

I watched in horror as the stoplight changed from green to yellow. I looked over at Jake. His eyes were locked on mine. He had stopped paying attention to the road. His attention was on me with no attention on the intersection that we sped towards.

The light turned red.

Time slowed down.

I saw and understood everything now. I could see Jake was one of those kids that was doomed before he ever got going with his life. The deck was stacked against him, and he decided he was going to make it more difficult on himself without even knowing about it.

I took my eyes away from Jake and the gun, and I saw the red light through the whooshing of the windshield wipers. It commanded us to stop. I looked back at him. All I could see was unrestrained fury directed at me. He was completely out of control now. I looked down at the gun and watched it complete its outward arc going away from his chest just before he redirected it and moved it back for another tap against his chest.

I looked up and over Jake's shoulder to see the headlights from a blue car coming right at us. I saw the woman behind the wheel as she stared in horror and swerved to her right, with her horn blaring, barely missing us.

I looked back at Jake as he went to tap the gun against his chest one last time. His eyes went wide as they flicked from my eyes to looking over my shoulder. I turned in my seat and saw the snow covering the hood of a big green truck inches from my window and closing fast.

Tap.

Bang! Bang!

EPILOGUE

Major things that happen in a person's life are rare things. You can go along smooth sailing for years, and then BAM! Something major happens that you are unprepared for. Or, sometimes, you can see where something is lurking just beyond the horizon. It is like a storm cloud approaching.

You can see it coming, but you cannot just tell it to go away. You still have to prepare yourself for what is coming.

Believe me. I know how something unexpected can change a person's life. I also know how a foreseeable event can change a person's life as well. How we handle these changes can shape your life for the present and for the future.

Normally, we have no power over these life-changing events. You learn to live or cope with these life-altering events. The fact is that we do not have a choice in what happens.

We have to deal with the events that face us whether we like it or not, or suffer the consequences.

As Jake learned, there are right and wrong ways to deal with life's twists and turns.

Over the next couple of weeks, I came to realize that some of these events had happened to me, but I had little knowledge of anything that had transpired.

I came to realize that I was in a hospital somewhere. The reason I was there took some time for me to figure out. I was in a haze for about what seemed like a month, but only lasted for a little over a day. My only fuzzy recollections were of doctors, family, and friends standing over my bed, speaking to me. I could remember nothing said to me for the first couple of days.

At some point, I figured out that my right leg was broken. The other leg was fine. Everywhere I went in the hospital, I had to travel by wheelchair with someone pushing me.

After the fourth or fifth day, I'm not sure which, I could start remembering things that others were trying to tell me. The first bit of knowledge I was able to hold on to was that I was in a car accident. I remembered nothing of being in a wreck, but my injuries proved otherwise to me.

The next thing that I could comprehend was that I had suffered a severe concussion in the accident along with a broken leg. The doctors said that the concussion had caused me to have some short-term memory loss. They also said that I was a very lucky young man, but would have to stay in the hospital for, they hoped, only three weeks.

When I asked for details of the accident, no one would tell me what exactly had happened.

As to the events before my accident, I remembered little of the few months before it happened. Elizabeth came to the hospital after the fourth day and informed me we had been dating for a couple of months. This astonished me. I could not see myself ever getting up the gall to ask her out.

She told me that if I could not remember what happened between us, not to worry about it. She said right after my accident her brother came home from college to check on how I was doing.

When he came, he brought his roommate with him. I searched my memory, and I thought I could recall that he and Elizabeth had a little thing going on during the previous summer. When Elizabeth saw him again, without knowing if I would ever be okay, and knowing that I remembered nothing about us having a relationship, she resumed their relationship.

I knew Elizabeth liked to 'play the field', so to speak. I always thought that her never-ending carousel of boyfriends was funny.

This was okay with me since I did not know we were dating, anyway. My other friends, Stone, Allen, Brian, Hunter, and others made appearances every couple of days. They were supportive of me and hoped I could join them back at school soon.

After the second week, they finally explained to me the circumstances of my accident. They told me about some guy named Jake, who I do not remember, and how he forced me into my car with a gun that he had stolen from Ashley's dad. There were reports after the accident of my car seen speeding through Summersville, out of control.

A big truck slammed into us in on the passenger side as we sped through the intersection of Main Street and Broad Street.

I was told that this Jake guy was the one driving, and I was on the side the truck hit causing the severe injuries I suffered. The driver of the truck ended up with a concussion and a totaled pickup. Jake did not have a scratch on him. However, the crash caused him to shoot himself in the chest, directly into his heart at the moment of impact.

He died immediately.

I could not imagine what would have led to me being in a car with a guy whom I don't remember meeting and him brandishing a gun at me. I would like to hear the story of how we came to be in that car together sometime.

When I asked for more details about this Jake guy, I was told that he and his family had moved into the neighborhood a few months prior to our car accident. Jake had bi-polar disorder, and the medication prescribed for him helped to keep him under control. Apparently, when he did not take his pills, he became unpredictable. They said that his mom found he had been hiding the spare pills under his bed, deceiving his parents into thinking that he was taking them every night before going to sleep.

There was a small, private memorial service for Jake at a small Baptist Church just outside of Summersville where they had the burial ceremony. Only his parents and a few of Jake's teachers attended. A week later, there was a For Sale sign in their front yard, and Jake's parents were gone from Summersville shortly thereafter.

I came to learn that even when my leg healed, I could never play sports to the ability I used to. The break that occurred in my leg was so severe that I would forever have a slight limp. They said my short-term memory loss would only be temporary until the swelling in that part of my brain fully subsided. They said I would probably never remember the weeks leading up to this accident. They told me this was the second severe concussion I suffered in the past few months, and if I suffered any more concussions, it might cause some severe, permanent damage.

Some events, they said, from the previous months may return to me, but made no promises.

The one bright spot—if there was a bright spot—was Ashley. She was at my side every day after the accident, and some mornings even before school started. On the weekends, she would sit by my bed the whole time. She would talk and read to me. She assured me that everything would be okay.

One day in between therapy sessions, my dad was wheeling me to the next room for therapy. He told me everything would be okay and if I were smart, I should try making a relationship with Ashley. It was something I remembered giving thought to in the past. He told me he had never seen someone show such dogged devotion to another.

On one cloudy day, I laid in the hospital bed alone, and thought about my dad's suggestion.

I asked Ashley one evening why she stayed by my bed. She said, with a tear in her eye, that it was because she loved me. When I asked her what had happened during the months leading up to my accident, she said it was not important right then and would someday tell me. She told me that if I wished for her to, she would remain by my side.

They released me from the hospital three weeks after they admitted me. I walked on crutches with my parents leading the way. My parents' car was parked out front. I had Ashley at my side.

I told her I wanted her to grant that wish.

READ MORE

Be sure to read the next installment in the Lucas Caine
Series,
A Murder in Concord!

Read Caleb's next mystery, *Death on the Boardwalk*
(Book 1 of The Myrtle Beach Mysteries)!

Enjoy this novel? Please consider leaving a review on
Amazon and/or Goodreads.

Learn more about Caleb and his books on his website,
CalebWygal.com.

ABOUT THE AUTHOR

Photo by Pamela Hartle

Caleb is a member of the Mystery Writers of America, The International Thriller Writers. and Southeastern Writers Association, Caleb has authored nine novels. He is a Mystery Writing instructor affiliated with the Osher Lifelong Learning Institution at Coastal Carolina University.

He's also a social media marketer, smoker of meats, amateur woodworker, occasional golfer, and a beach enthusiast known for his knack for not finding shark teeth along the shoreline. In his Lucas Caine Adventure series, Caleb's novels, *Blackbeard's Lost Treasure* and *The Search for the Fountain of Youth,* earned the distinction of being Semi-Finalists in the Clive Cussler Adventure Awards Competition.

Currently immersed in crafting the next installment of the Myrtle Beach Mystery Series, Caleb resides in Myrtle Beach with his loving wife and son. His passion for unraveling mysteries and teaching the art of mystery writing continues to inspire aspiring writers and captivate readers worldwide.